I0672827

Super Gremlin 2

King Rio

Lock Down Publications and Ca$h
Presents
Super Gremlin 2
A Novel by *King Rio*

King Rio

Lock Down Publications
Po Box 944
Stockbridge, Ga 30281

Visit our website @
www.lockdownpublications.com

Copyright 2023 by King Rio
Super Gremlin 2

All rights reserved. No part of this book may be reproduced in any form or by electronic or mechanical means, including information storage and retrieval systems without permission in writing from the publisher, except by a reviewer who may quote brief passages in review.
First Edition June 2023
Printed in the United States of America

This is a work of fiction. Names, characters, places, and incidents either are products of the author's imagination or are used fictitiously. Any similarity to actual events or locales or persons, living or dead, is entirely coincidental.

Lock Down Publications
Like our page on Facebook: Lock Down Publications @
www.facebook.com/lockdownpublications.ldp
Book interior design by: **Shawn Walker**
Edited by: **Nuel Uyi**

Stay Connected with Us!

Text **LOCKDOWN** to 22828 to stay up-to-date with new releases,
sneak peaks, contests and more...
Thank you.

Submission Guideline.

Submit the first three chapters of your completed manuscript to ldpsubmissions@gmail.com, subject line: Your book's title. The manuscript must be in a .doc file and sent as an attachment. Document should be in Times New Roman, double spaced and in size 12 font. Also, provide your synopsis and full contact information. If sending multiple submissions, they must each be in a separate email.

Have a story but no way to send it electronically? You can still submit to LDP/Ca$h Presents. Send in the first three chapters, written or typed, of your completed manuscript to:

LDP: Submissions Dept
Po Box 944
Stockbridge, Ga 30281

DO NOT send original manuscript. Must be a duplicate.

Provide your synopsis and a cover letter containing your full contact information.

Thanks for considering LDP and Ca$h Presents.

Acknowledgements

First and foremost, I'd like to say thank you to Ca$h and the entire Lockdown Publications team for partnering with me on this literary journey. I'd also like to thank my cousin Devario Lewis for being my eyes and ears while I'm away from social media, and every reader who continued to support me through the decade of my writing career. I truly do appreciate every single one of you.

For those who wish to know the chronological order of my novels, I suggest you first read The Cocaine Princess series, then Mobbed Up books 1 through 4, then The Brick Man books 1 through 5, and finally the Super Gremlin series (which is, I must say, the absolute BEST urban fiction series I've ever written!).

Free the bros. Free me. And God bless.

King Rio

Prologue

July 6th, 2022—11:30 PM

Whitney Clarrett was all cried out.

She'd been at it for more than an hour, crying and sobbing, weeping and waiting, until her tear ducts gave up and closed for business. She'd gone through almost an entire box of Kleenex tissues, wiping her eyes and blowing her nose and then doing it all over again. She was sitting Indian style on her bed, wearing the red lace Savage X Fenty bra and red silk pajamas shorts she put on after soaking in a nice hot bubble bath, which she had taken right after she and her kids got the house put back together.

Every bedroom had been thoroughly searched—clothes from drawers emptied into the floor, beds flipped over, closets rummaged through. It looked like the police had executed a search warrant at 302 E Comb Street, but Whitney knew what really had happened.

The Chicago boys had broken in and searched for the eight stainless steel suitcases. Not that she blamed them. After all, if she had stashed $5 million inside of eight steel suitcases and then lost it to some dumb storage auction, she'd go through hell and high water to recover it herself.

Whitney heard laughter and loud conversation coming from her son's upstairs bedroom. Seventeen-year-old James Thomas junior, better known as Lil' Jimmy, had invited two of his high school friends to stay the night, as well as his girlfriend—Crystal. All four of the them were in possession of legally owned firearms, even though the chief of police had stationed an officer right outside the house just in case the burglars returned.

Two of Whitney's teenage daughters were spending the night with their aunt—Candace. Her thirteen-year-old daughter, Eva, was at the Juvenile Detention Center, waiting to go to court in the morning so she could be released. She and Whitney had both gotten arrested for assaulting the woman who'd followed them after being offered $50,000 to track down the person who bought the five-million-dollar storage locker. After bonding out of jail, Whitney had been forced to shoot and kill a Draco-tatted gunman who jumped out on her and demanded she get in the car with him. Which had landed her back in police custody for an hour-long interrogation, only to return home and find that her place had been burglarized. And to top it all off, her boyfriend of the last sixteen months had just dumped her after learning she'd had an affair with one of his close friends a few years back. They hadn't been together at the time, but he was upset that she hadn't told him about it. And since he had the eight suitcases, she couldn't risk fighting with him about the breakup.

Today had been one hell of a day.

Someone knocked at Whitney's bedroom door. Three raps, sharp and quick.

Thump-thump-thump.

She looked up from her iPhone, on which she'd been perusing her Instagram page, looking at all the photos and videos she'd taken with Markio Earl, the handsome man who'd been all hers until a few hours ago.

"Yeah?" Whitney said.

"It's me, Ms. Clarrett. Flocka. You OK in there?"

Eighteen-year-old Aaron Fellows, better known as Flocka, was Lil' Jimmy's best friend.

Whitney had never allowed any of her children's friends into her bedroom, but right now she needed somebody—anybody.

"Yeah," she said. "I'm fine. You can come in."

He turned the knob and pushed the door halfway open, and after watching her dab at her red-rimmed eyes with a damp wipe of tissue, he stepped into the bedroom. Flocka was a big boy, six feet three inches tall and about two hundred and sixty pounds of youthful muscle. He was pecan brown and wore a yellow Adidas shirt that hugged his muscular torso like a long-lost relative. His yellow Adidas sweatshirts had drawstrings tied at the front, just above a notable bulge where his dick should be. His legs were long and powerful-looking. His long dreadlocks were pulled back in a knot, making his concerned eyes the center of attention.

"You still in here cryin' over that nigga?" He sat down next to her and put an arm around her shoulders, and before she knew it he had pulled her tight against his rock-hard chest. He smelled like weed and pizza and some kind of masculine cologne. His hair smelled like honey. "I don't mean to cuss in front of you, Ms. Clarrett, but fuck that nigga. He got to be the stupidest man on earth to leave somebody as beautiful as you."

Flocka was right, and Whitney knew it. She was a dime piece, a yellow bone with an exceptionally pretty face, long dark hair, and a body so curvaceous that a lot of people believe she had gotten it surgically thickened in places. Whitney was thirty-five, but she looked twenty-five. Her waist was small—just twenty-six inches around, and her ass was fat, her thighs thick, her hips jutting out like an old Coke bottle.

When Flocka loosened his grip on her a moment later, she kept her head on his shoulder, watching his reflection in the mirror behind her dresser. He looked genuinely concerned, but she could feel something else, too. Something simmering beneath their concern.

Something sexual.

What am I thinking? This boy is eighteen years old, and I'll be thirty-six next weekend. Twice his age, old enough to be his mother.

But the hole in her overrode common sense. The hole in her said, *This boy is eighteen, and eighteen is grown.* Plus, the bulge in the front of Flocka's shorts was growing so rapidly. She turned her head so she could look straight down at it instead of gazing at him in the mirror, and then she reached down and squeezed the impressive bulge. It felt fat in her hands, like an overweight python.

The girth was what did it for her—well, that and the notion that she could probably talk Flocka into breaking into Markio's house to steal the suitcase if Markio didn't cut her in on that five million dollars.

She got up and went to shut and lock her door, then flicked the light off and turned to face Flocka in the darkness. He had already stood and removed his shirt, tossing it aside. As she walked to him, he took her by the waist and lifted her off her feet, wrapping her

11

legs around his waist and kissing her; his kisses were rough, passionate. He sucked and licked on her lips, and then his tongue was in her mouth, darting in and out. He turned and laid her on the bed, his kisses moving down to her neck.

"Jimmy gon' kill us," he said with a light chuckle.

Whitney had no response to that. She began removing her shorts. Flocka took a moment to suck on her toes, and as soon as her shorts were off, he went down between her legs and stuck his tongue in her pussy, a tongue that felt longer than some dicks she'd had in her. He'd apparently not yet learned that he was supposed lick on a woman's clitoris to make her come, but his tongue felt too good inside of her to correct him, so Whitney relaxed and rubbed her fingertips on her clit while Flocka tongue-fucked her pussy.

Well, the next four or five minutes she just let him lick and lick while she held his knotted dreads and massaged her clitoris in a fast, circular motion. Then he went down a little further and dug that perilously long tongue into her asshole, and within seconds she was coming all over his mouth.

Flocka lapped the juices that trickled down into her ass crack. He closed his mouth around her quivering labia and slurped up all he could, drinking thirstily.

Whitney was still shivering through the orgasm when Flocka rose to his knees and snatched down his shorts. His dick sprang out, bobbing up and down, fat and black and leaking precum. It wasn't as long as Markio's but it was definitely thicker, so thick that Whitney gasped and held her breath as she eased the fat cockhead in between her slippery vaginal lips.

She sucked in an even deeper breath as he pushed his weight in, stretching her walls to the limit. He began with slow, short strokes. Whitney dug her fingernails into the flesh of his forearms, loving the way the moonlight spilled in through her window and illuminated Flocka's intensively muscled chest and arms. As his strokes became faster and longer, he leaned in and clamped one hand around her throat, making it difficult for her to breathe—difficult, but not impossible. The pressure around her neck was a turn-on she'd never experienced. It made her so wet that there were splashing sounds as he slid in and out of her.

From upstairs came another roar of laughter. Jimmy, his girlfriend, and his other friend—Melvo "Mellie Mel" Crenshaw—were having a blast doing something. Their laughter could not have come at a more opportune time, because at that very moment Whitney dropped her head back and let out a piercing moan as her body seized up in yet another soul-shaking orgasm.

Flocka kept at it a while longer—the boy had stamina—and then pulled his fat dick out of her and sprayed her tight abdomen with hot white semen. Afterward, he stayed in position, kneeling between her parted thighs, stroking his softening love muscle and squeezing out the last few drops of pungent cum until a knock on the bedroom door froze them both in place.

"Mama." It was Lil' Jimmy.

"Yeah?" Whitney answered.

"Flocka came down here a minute ago and I can't find him. He didn't happen to tell you where he was goin', did he?"

"Umm—yeah, to the gas station. He walked to the gas station for something."

"Ma, you know my daddy never even came up to the hospital to see me?"

"I'm trying to sleep, Jimmy."

"Oh, my bad. Goodnight, Ma."

Whitney listened closely to Lil' Jimmy's retreating footfalls. As he left from outside her door, she reached for the box of Kleenex and was wiping the sticky cum off her belly when Flocka went down on her again. Her eyebrows shot up in surprise, but she didn't say a word as he left his tongue deep in her pussy, slurping and licking. He slipped a forefinger into her asshole as she began massaging her clitoris. This time she was wise enough to turn on some music and up the volume before she got to moaning. Now if Jimmy walked up to her door, all he'd hear is Ari Lennox singing "Pressure."

Suddenly, Whitney had no regrets about hooking up with Flocka. She needed him in case Markio didn't cut her in on the cash he'd gotten from that storage locker—from the storage auction *she* had suggested they go to—and if this was what Flocka had in store for her until then, she didn't have a single complaint.

Chapter One

When Markio woke up the following morning on his close friend Reggie's living room sofa, the first thing he did was check his iPhone. The time was just 7:05 a.m. and already he had ten new text messages.

One text was from his parole officer, Terry Pratchett, who wanted him to call her; she said it was urgent. Two messages were from Loochie, a weed-dealer who wanted to stop by and pick up the pound of gelato Markio was supposed to have sold him yesterday. The rest of the text messages were from people gossiping about all the shootings that had taken place in the last twenty-four hours. There hadn't been four murders in one day since the day of Blake "Bulletface" King, the multi platinum gangster rapper who was the only real international success story to ever come out of Michigan City, Indiana. Markio was in prison at the time, but he'd heard all about it, mostly from celebrity news shows like *TMZ* and *Extra*.

Markio sat up and yawned. He needed to wash his face and brush his teeth, and he knew Reggie would have clean towels and new toothbrushes in the bathroom. Reggie had left his Micro Draco machine pistol lying on the coffee table, and Markio picked it up and carried it to the bathroom with him, despite the fact that he already had a .45 caliber Ruger stuck down in his Amiri jeans.

After taking care of his hygiene, Markio sat at the kitchen table and poured himself a big bowl of Kellogg's frosted flakes. He dialed his mother's phone number and set his phone and the Draco down next to his bowl.

"Good morning," Jeanette answered in her usually cheerful tone.

"Good morning, Mama. The hell you doin' up so early?"

"Drinkin' my coffee and watchin' the news. These niggas been shooting like crazy out here. You know it's bad when they talkin' about it on the South Bend news and the Chicago news. One boy got killed right over there on 7th Street. Taquisha say his name was P. Money or something like that. Say they blew his damn brains out."

Markio chuckled. "G-Money, Mama," he corrected. "Look, I need you to get a couple of bags packed. I'm sending you and Taquisha on a lil' vacation."

"A vacation? To where?"

"Wherever y'all wanna go. I got eight thousand dollars for you and the same for her."

"Whaaat?" She laughed the high pitched laugh she reserved for these few instances of real-deal excitement. "Okaaaay. When do we leave?"

"As soon as you can get dressed and ready. You don't need to pack too much. Y'all can just buy a lot of stuff new, and if you run through that eight thousand I'll send you some more money. Just try to hurry up."

Jeanette paused, and Markio could almost see her toothless, pink-gum smile. She owned a set of dentures, but she hated wearing them because she said they hurt her gums. Mama was sixty-five years young, her gray hair going on white with age, but she was still as lively and humorous as ever.

"Okay," she said, after a while. "Let me finish this coffee and call Taquisha. You know your brother and his wife went to Aruba not too long ago. I think that's where I wanna go."

"A'ight, I'll be over there in about thirty minutes."

"Okay. Bring me a pack of cigarettes."

Markio ended the call and ate his cereal in silence as he thought over his current troubles. He had two enemies he absolutely *had* to get rid of: Leezo, a Gangster Disciple from the Inglewood neighborhood on the South side of Chicago; and Big Worm, a heroin kingpin and high-ranking Traveling Vice Lord from Markio's North Lawndale hood on Chicago's West side.

Leezo wanted Markio dead out of retaliation for the murder of Gregory "G-Money" Samuels. He'd somehow figured out that Markio was the masked gunman who ran down on G-Money yesterday afternoon and shot him in the face. As soon as Markio got word that Leezo and his gang wanted him dead, he'd put $20,000 on each of their heads, and two of their own fellow GD's had snaked them for the money, killing Polo and D-Nut, two of Leezo's closest gang members. Markio hadn't heard anything from Leezo since, but he knew Lezzo was from Tookaville, one of the most treacherous hoods in Chicago, so he expected Leezo to pop out on him sooner or later, and it wouldn't be to have a conversation.

Big Worm, the man whose money Markio had gotten from the storage auction, had learned that it was Markio who actually had the cash. Which wouldn't have meant much had Markio not grown up around Worm and his family in North Lawndale, where a large portion of Markio's father's side of the family still resided. Worm knew that Markio was in Michigan City, and he also knew that Markio's sister Taquisha lived here. With Mama and Taquisha out of town, Markio could focus on taking care of both Leezo and Worm.

And with five million dollars in the eight suitcases he'd stashed away in the bedroom he still had at his mother's place, Markio felt he had more than enough money to deal with his enemies.

He finished his cereal and went to the double basin sink to wash the bowl and put it away. He was rinsing out the bowl when he heard the sound of a toilet flushing, and Reggie joined him in the kitchen a minute later.

Reggie was as black as charcoal, and always as clean as the twenty gold teeth in his mouth. He entered the kitchen wearing a dark blue Versace bathrobe, brushing the waves in his hair. Markio had waves too, but his didn't spin all the way around his head the way Reggie's did. But then again, up until yesterday, Markio's savings had amounted to a little over 30 grand, while Reggie easily pocketed six figures off every trip he made to California with a pick-up-the-loads-of-high-grade-marijuana he sold.

"Where in the fuck did you get all that money?" Reggie asked, picking a box of chocolate chip granola bars from the top of his stainless steel refrigerator. He'd seen the massive piles of hundreds Markio had on him last night, but he hadn't mentioned it until now.

"Got it from the storage auction. That's why Worm paid them niggas to come out here and find his suitcases," Markio said, taking a fresh pack of Newports out of his pocket and pinching out one cigarette to light. "He got shot up in April, and was in a coma for almost three months. I guess he put all his money in the storage locker before he got shot, and since he didn't pay the bill they auctioned it off. I just happened to be the one who bought it."

"And it just happened to belong to a nigga you know from Chicago."

"I know, right? Small world." Markio puffed on his cigarette and blew a stream of smoke at his smartphone as he lifted it from the table. The screen was lighting up with a call from his parole officer. "Shit. This my PO calling."

"Aww shit," Reggie said and left the kitchen as quickly as he entered it, apparently wanting nothing more to do with the criminal justice system. Reluctantly, Markio answered the call, and Terry Pratchett set right in.

"I don't know what the hell you've managed to get yourself into, but you better get a damn good lawyer," she said. "The police are urging me to find a violation to bring you in on until they can gather enough evidence to charge you with murder. Chief Swiztek has called me twice already. He wants me to violate you for that shooting at the Marriott last night. They have you on camera with a gun in your hand."

"Yeah, again I picked up off the floor after—"

"I know, I know I saw the footage. The guy pointed a gun at you, Mya Patterson shot him. He shot you in the leg, and you picked up his gun after he dropped it to keep his partner at bay. I can't violate you for that."

"Then what I need a lawyer for?"

"You need a lawyer because your name has come up at least three times in two different homicide investigations. Jermaine McCoy, one of the men who was shot and killed in front of the house on Cedar St. last night, had just called in a tip saying you were the shooter behind Gregory Samuels' murder yesterday afternoon, and two of the people police spoke with at the scene of last night's double murder mentioned you as a possible suspect. They said the two victims—Dennis Carter and Germaine McCoy— had been talking about getting back at you for allegedly killing Samuels right before they were gunned down on the front porch."

"I was at the Marriott when that happened."

"I know. Just get yourself a lawyer if you can afford one, period. You still working?"

"Yeah. Part time at Johnson Brothers Roofing. I worked Monday, and I gotta go in tomorrow and Saturday," Markio lied. Truthfully, Maurice Johnson, the owner of the roofing company, had put Markio on the payroll as a favor, so that he would have proof of income for parole. "I'll see what my check looks like this week. I might have enough for a lawyer. My family will help me."

"OK." Pratchett was quiet for a couple of seconds; then: "One more thing."

"What?" Markio picked up the Draco and left the kitchen for the living room.

"You did get shot in the elevator, right?"

"Yup." Markio looked down at the dime sized hole in the right side of his black Amiri jeans.

"It didn't go all the way through, did it? You had something in your pocket that stopped the bullet."

"I definitely have something in my pocket," Markio said, and laughed.

He used the Draco to push the vertical blinds over the living room window aside and peered out into the front yard. Reggie lived in a good neighborhood, in a predominantly white section of town about fourteen blocks southwest of Markio's home. There were no rundown trap houses on this street, no prostitutes walking up and down the sidewalks with their eyes thirstily trained on every passing vehicle.

"So what was it?" Pratchett asked. "I'm curious. What could you have possibly had in your pocket that was strong enough to stop a bullet?"

A cocky grin raised one corner of Markio's mouth. "I plead the 5th," he said, and hung up, conscious of the fact that the hang up was a bit rude and perhaps not the wisest thing to do to the woman who could easily have him sent back to prison, but too eager to make the next phone call to give a damn.

He had to call Mya Patterson, the woman who saved his life in that hotel elevator last night—the woman who was Herman "Big Worm" Patterson's youngest sister.

Chapter Two

Mya Patterson, the twenty-one year old redbone who'd fallen in love with Markio Earl at first sight, was dozing in her claw foot bathtub, her diminutive body submerged from the neck beneath the jasmine-scented bubbles, when her iPhone chimed with a *FaceTime* call from Markio. She'd picked it up from the chromium tray she connected to the side of her bathtub and inhaled a deep, nervous breath before she answered.

When his handsome face appeared on the screen, she exhaled the breath and regarded him with a look of intense scrutiny, her eyes squinted, her pretty mouth shifted to one side of her pretty face.

"Thanks," Markio said.

"Mm-hmm."

He chuckled at her attitude. "Damn. What was that for?"

"You could have told me that gun was stolen. I got charged for that, period. Now I have to hire a lawyer and see if I can get the charge dismissed."

"I'll pay for the lawyer. My parole officer just told me I need to get a lawyer for myself, so I'll just hire one for both of us." He sat down on a black leather sofa and raised the cigarette to his mouth. "Tell me what the police said when they got there."

"Lil' Mark is still alive. I shot him seven times in the stomach, chest, and hip. He's on life support, but they said there is a chance he could survive. I pray to God he does. I can't have that on my conscience. I might play tough but I'm really sensitive as fuck."

"He would have killed me if you hadn't shot him."

"Yeah, I know. But I grew up around him. I know all his family. His sister Portia was one of my best friends, but I just had to block her on Instagram. That crazy bitch got in my comments talkin' about what she gon' do to me when she catch me. I don't do all that social media drama. I'm way too pretty to be fightin' hoes, but I'll shoot the fuck out that bitch. Have her laid up in the same room with her brother." Mya sucked her teeth, her eyelids narrowing again. "Wait a minute, though. You need to tell me why my brother paid Pee Wee and Lil' Mark to come at you in the first place. How did you end up with his money? And why didn't you tell me about it when I told you Worm was one of my big brothers?"

Markio took a long moment to respond. He blew smoke at the camera. He glanced at something off-screen. He ran his hand over his waves and grinned as he stared into Mya's eyes. And just when she was about to clear her throat and scream at him through the phone, he spoke.

"I went to a storage auction yesterday morning. Needed some furniture for my new place, and Whitney talked me into checkin' out the auction. Worm's locker was the second one they showed. As soon as I saw the leather couches and the bedroom set, I was locked in. I paid a thousand dollars for the locker, and I didn't know what was actually in the suitcases until you knocked 'em over in my bedroom. When you went to the bathroom, I started picking the suitcase back up. One of 'em fell open, and a bunch of money spilled out."

"How much money was it?"

"Ask your brother."

"He won't tell me. I asked him after I left the police station last night. All he kept saying was *it's gon' be hell for you if he don't get it back.*"

Following another pause, this one much shorter than the last, Markio said, "I hope you didn't tell that nigga—"

"Don't say it, Markio. Don't even think about it. I would not dare give him your address. I'm not that type of bitch. I don't get involved in nothin' my brothers got going on in the streets. Star won't get involved, either. Your address is safe with us."

Mya could see the relief wash over Markio's face. The slight smile she'd fallen in love with three days ago returned. He licked his lips and began looking toward the bottom of the screen.

"Get up out that tub. Let me see them goodies," he said.

Mya rolled her eyes, biting down on her bottom lip. An incoming text alert made her phone buzz in her hand, but she ignored it and rose up out of the water. Another text alert came in as she was stepping out of the bathtub. Frustrated, she sighed and wiped the notification bar down to see who texted her, and she saw it was her brother Worm.

"I'll give you one million if you can help me get that money back from Markio."

Mya ended the call abruptly and dried herself up in somewhat of a daze, her young adult mind swirling in the tornado of numbers, mostly the seven-figure offer from Worm and also the visually appealing number of high-end designer shoes and purses she could instantly purchase with a million dollars in cash.

She made it out of her personal bathroom and into the adjoining bedroom. There were seven bedrooms and twelve bathrooms in the Victorian-style lakefront mansion, and no one but the maid and Mya's older sister—Star—ever entered her bedroom, so she was comfortable walking around in the nude.

But she wasn't nude for long. She moisturized her skin, deodorized, and then dressed hurriedly in a powder blue Celine bodysuit over strappy white Balenciaga heels. The Gucci shoulder bag she'd worn last night had a gaping hole in one side—she had fired the stolen MK10 from inside the bag when she shot Lil' Mark in the hotel elevator—so she dumped everything out of it and replaced it all inside a white leather Celine bag. She took a couple of minutes applying her cosmetics, and then she was out the door.

She didn't have far to walk. Her Big Brothers—Leroy "Bam" Patterson and Herman "Big Worm" Patterson—were in the foyer, getting ready to leave, when she came walking down the butterfly staircase.

"Where are y'all going?" Mya asked.

The two giant men turned to look at her. They were both well over 6 feet tall. The coma had shed a good 30 pounds off Worm's chubby frame, but he was still fat and round. Bam was in much better shape, wearing an all black Amiri outfit and about a million dollars' worth of jewelry. He smiled at Mya, and the diamonds that covered all of his front teeth twinkled back magically in the early morning sunlight.

"Lil' sister!" Bam said, excited as always to see his baby sister.

Mya didn't reciprocate the excitement. She walked right up to Worm and crossed her arms over her chest. His left arm was still in a cast from the shooting that had landed him in a coma for three months, but aside from that he looked fine.

"A million dollars?" Mya said, looking up at Worm.

"That's what I said, ain't it?"

Mya exhaled nasally and stuck out her bottom lip. She was thinking. Her mother, Jesse Mae, made over a million every year from Gold Express, the trucking company she owned in Chicago, but after tax deductions, insurance, payroll, and the many other expenses that made up the business overhead, she ended up with just two or three hundred thousand dollars property taxes, and maintenance cost on her two million dollar mansion ate into that, and the rest she spent shopping and traveling the globe. She'd give Mya and Star a few grand every now and then, but for the most part they had to fend for themselves. Star was now a phlebotomist at Saint Anthony's Hospital, bringing in $115,000 a year, and Mya made decent money as a real estate agent, but no one in the Patterson mansion had a million dollars to their name.

Worm and Bam, both of whom still live in Chicago, were the only true millionaires in the family, and all their millions came from dealing heroin. They were the ones who footed the bill for Mya's high-end fashion addiction. Worm was tight with his money; getting a few grand from him was about as easy as wrestling with a grizzly bear. But Bam splurged on his sisters. He'd given Mya $50,000 on her birthday and another $50,000 when she received her real estate license.

Mya walked up to Bam and gave him a hug, still looking at Worm out of the corner of her eye, trying to decide if his million dollar offer was worth betraying Markio Earl.

***

"Folks, on Tooka grave, when I catch this hoe ass nigga Markio, I'm killin' him. If either one of y'all go out and hear about a

Traveler named Markio, get on his ass. I got ten thousand on his head."

The other eight Tookaville Gangster Disciples seated around the small living room inside Tamisha Robinson's apartment turned to look at Leezo.

Tamisha, the mother of Lezzo's ten-year-old daughter Aleyah, lived in the apartment building located at 6428 S Lowe on the South side of Chicago, in the Englewood neighborhood where Leezo and most of his family were born and raised. Peppermint wasn't a regular hangout spot for the gang whenever Leezo was in town. He left the city after learning that one of his opps had put a $100,000 price tag on his head, but he always came back, when he felt it was safe.

A dense haze of marijuana smoke clouded the room. There were five blunts of exotic in rotation, and all the guys had cups filled with ice cubes, creme soda, and promethazine.

"Where he from? Out west?" asked Wooski, the most successful member of the gang. He was a popular trill rapper who put on for the Tookavilla GD's in every one of his songs. Every member of the gang—known to some as the "Getcha Shit Splat" gang—they committed at least one murder in their years-long war with the 300 Black Disciples, and Wooski was one of the deadliest gangsters in the city, often standing over his opps and shooting them twenty or thirty times in the head before running back to his vehicle and speeding off into the night.

Leezo shrugged. "Somewhere out west. That's all I know. He's been in Indiana for some years but he originally from out West."

"What he do?" Wooki's question came out slurred. He'd suffered a gunshot wound to his head during the fellow gang member Dooki's funeral service a few years back, and the injury had affected his speech.

"He got D-Nut and my little nigga Polo whacked last night," Leezo said, coughing repeatedly as he handed Muskie the blunt. "He nailed one of the folks from Harvey yesterday, too. One of the folks I fucked with heavy—my nigga G-Money."

"If he did all that in Indiana yesterday, then that's probably where you need to be looking for him." Wooski looked down at the .40 caliber Glock 22 he had resting on his lap. The gun had a switch that modified it to fully automatic, as well as fifty round drum magazine and a red laser sighting. "You wanna slide back out there now? We can't hit the highway. I'm with it. On Tooka. I really wanted to slide on O Block and see if we can catch one of them bitch ass BD's outside, but you know them bitch-ass ain't coming from behind that fence."

Leezo picked up his own Glock. His point-40 caliber Glock 23 only had a 30-round extended clip, but he had two more 30-round clips in his pocket, and his Glock was also modified with a switch. Wooski had just given him the gun and the two extra clips. TuTu, another member of the gang, had a Mac 11 strapped around his neck. Next to Tutu, Fat Head sat with a Tec-9 on his lap, rolling another blunt. Altogether, there were ten guns in the room, and Leezo still had a Heckler & Koch MP5 and an AR15 outside of his pickup truck, the guns he picked up off the porch after Polo and D-Nut were killed.

The whole reason Leezo had left Michigan City last night was to get around his own game, the gangsters he was familiar with, because he had a nagging feeling that one of the genies in Michigan City had snaked him. How else could Markio have figured out where to find them last night? How could he have known when exactly to catch Polo and D-Nut standing out on the front porch? No one outside of his circle had known that information; well, no one aside from Polo's girlfriend Tandra, her friend Lisa, and a sexy ass black and Puerto Rican girl named Valerie.

"Man, fuck all that," said Lil' Jay, a dark-skinned GD with long dreads and an even longer list of murder victims. "Let's do both. I say we slide down O-Block and light that bitch up. Then we slide down Lamron and light *that* bitch up. Then we drive to Indiana, find that nigga Markio and light *his* bitch-ass up."

Leezo cracked a sinister smile. "That's it right there, Folks," he said with a nod.

The plan was set.

***

The time was 8:37 a.m. when Bam pulled up to the wrought-iron gates at the front of Bankroll Reese's ten- million-dollar mansion. Situated on a prominent intersection in the exclusive Chicago suburb of Burr Ridge, the 30,000 square foot home had a Jerusalem limestone exterior. The interior, appointed in Brazilian wood and Italian marble, featured nine fireplaces, a 24-seat theater, and a high ceilinged ballroom.

The fat black man in the guard shack looked into Bam's blacked-out Rolls-Royce Cullinan, saw that it was only Bam and Worm inside the luxury SUV, and pressed a button that sent the ten-foot gates swinging inward.

"Mama crib ain't got shit on this," Worm said, ogling the facade of the enormous mansion as Bam accelerated up the long flower-lined cobblestone driveway. "This muhfucka *huge*."

"They call it the Villa Taj," said Bam. "Eleven bedrooms. Indoor basketball courts. A pool with a fifteen-foot water slide. A twenty-car underground garage. I *Googled* it when he first bought it back in 2016. R Kelly used to live here."

Big Worm scratched at the side of his neck and stared straight ahead. The 30-milligram Oxycodone pills he'd popped to get rid of the pain of his surgery scars had him on cloud nine, but they made him itch like a flea-ridden puppy. He had changed into gray Dior joggers with matching sneakers. Like his brother, Worm had stuffed his pockets with blue-faced hundred and put on all his diamond Cuban-link bracelets and necklaces. Bam had switched out his Amiri outfit for a Versace shirt and shorts set. They weren't nearly as wealthy as Reese, but they were millionaires just like him.

Well, at least Bam was a millionaire.

Worm had been a millionaire until Markio got hold of his suitcases yesterday morning. Now all he had was the money he'd stuffed in his pockets, exactly $88,000 in rubber-banded Benjamins.

There were four vehicles parked in the circular drive in front of the Villa Taj—a Bugatti Veyron, a Rolls Royce Phantom, a

Lamborghini Aventador, and Bentley Bentayga. All four of the luxury vehicles were painted blood-red and shined to perfection.

And standing next to the Bentley truck was Bankroll Reese, along with his two longtime bodyguards, Suwu and Chubb.

Reese's jewelry was on par with Bam's, with several Cuban-links and glistening diamond pendants hanging down from his neck. Worm could see from thirty feet away that they iced out the one Bam had on. The black business suits Chubb and Suwu wore looked like they were ripped from the pages of GQ magazine, with red silk neckties and pocket squares and red croc skin shoes.

Bam parked beside the Bentayga. When he and Worm got out, Reese led the way into the mansion without uttering a single word. Suwu and Chubb trailed them inside, extinguishing Worm's fantasy of shooting Reese in the back of the head. He'd always loved Bankroll Reese like family, but the fact remained that Reese was Markio's cousin, and right now Worm wanted every living being related to Markio resting in a casket.

They took a left turn and went down a long hallway lined with doors on both sides. Reese cut into the third door on the right, and Worm entered behind him to find a massive entertainment room.

Against the left wall there was a giant 100-inch television that showed a paused game of *Black Ops: Modern Warfare 2* on the high-definition screen. A Playstation 5 game console sat alone on a shelf below the TV. Multiple game controllers were strewn across a gray marble table, and there were five thick leather reclining chairs positioned in a semicircle around the table. There was a second, identical setting directly next to the first one that looked unused, the television powered off, the controllers neatly placed on the table.

On the right side of the room, four pool tables were lined up side by side, spaced six feet apart, and the walls on that side were lined with large televisions showing half a dozen different sports channels. There was a fully-stocked bar at the back of the room with enough hard liquor behind the counter to supply a nightclub.

They took to the leather armchairs in front of the paused video game. Suwu remained standing, his right hand clasped around his left wrist just above his waistline, a stance that showed his allegiance to the Almighty Vice Lord nation without even having to say it.

"So what happened?" Reese asked, moving forward to the edge of his chair. "Why in the fuck am I hearing that y'all niggas done sent Lil' Mark and Baby Lord on a dummy mission and got 'em shot up? Pee Wee called Poochie from the county jail out there and told her your sister Mya shot up Lil' Mark last night. He said Ace got killed, and Baby Lord got shot and arrested. And now you call me talkin' about you having a problem with my cousin?"

"He got my money," Worm said. "Five million dollars of it. I want it back."

"Markio got five million dollars of your money? First off, how in the fuck was he even able to get it? Cuz ain't been to Chicago but once since he got out of the joint."

"It's a long story," Worm said, his teeth clenched tightly together.

"Well, it's gon' be a long day, 'cause I wanna hear all that."

Big Worm released a heated sigh of frustration. He felt like lashing out at Bankroll Reese, but he was in no condition to do such a thing. And he was almost too embarrassed to admit that he'd foolishly stored the cash in the storage locker before he was shot.

Bam sat forward and spoke for him.

"He had it in a storage locker in Michigan City. Markio and some bitch he fuck with—by the name of Whitney—went to the storage auction yesterday morning and bought it. Brah was in a coma for three months and nobody made the payments, so the storage place put his locker up for auction. Markio just happened to buy it."

"The night I got shot up was supposed to be my last night in Chicago," Worm explained. "I was moving to Michigan City to retire from the dope game. You know I had already got robbed and shot a couple of times before. Plus, the feds had just indicted the breeds and locked a bunch of them up. I wasn't tryin' to be next. I was gon' stay at my mama crib until I found my own place. That's why I had all my money in the storage locker. I was about to leave."

"You mean to tell me—you have *five million dollars—In cash*—in a fuckin' *storage locker?*"

Reese reclined to his chair and activated the massage feature, shaking his head, as he processed the details of what happened in his intelligent young brain. "*Anybody* could have bought that locker. You can't blame my cousin for that, nigga. That was an auction. Nigga, that man ain't stole shit from you. He bought that ship fair and square."

Worm said nothing. Had he spoken up his mind at the moment, Suwu might have pulled the gun and shot him dead.

"We need that bread back, Reese," said Bam. "That ain't no chump change. You got money. Give your big cousin a million or two so we can get past this bullshit and get back to the money."

Reese shook his head. "I'll call and highlight cuzzo, but I ain't gettin involved. That's between y'all." He pulled out his smartphone, looking from Bam to Worm and back to Bam again. "I'm tellin' y'all right now, though, if anything happens to my cousin…"

He trailed off, drawing his lips tight, his jaw muscles flexing as he looked Worm in the eye.

The threat was clear. The Earl family and the Patterson family both had a great number of outstanding gang members in their ranks, many of whom resided in North Lawndale. If Markio was harmed in any way, it could kick off a war between fellow gang members who've been close for decades, gang members who've been through numerous bullet wars with other gangs and lived to tell the next generation about it.

Bam pulled himself up from the armchair and went over to help Worm to his feet. The two of them shot one last glance at Bankroll Reese, then Suwu escorted them back out to their vehicle, neither of them speaking until they were seated in the Cullinan.

"Let's think this shit through," Bam said, starting the engine.

"Ain't shit to think about," Worm replied. "It's up there. Let's make the first move."

Chapter Three

"Sixty-fourth and King Drive, just outside the entrance to the Parkway Gardens apartment complex, where two young men were shot and killed and three others were wounded after several gunmen chased after them and opened fire not even thirty minutes ago. Both deceased victims were shot multiple times in the head in what police are calling a case of blatant overkill. Witnesses describe the getaway vehicle as being a black Buick Regal with a damaged front bumper and a silver, newer model Chevy Silverado—"

The description of the Silverado caught Markio's attention. He looked up from his phone. He was sitting in the waiting area at the Law Offices of Bostic and Staples, a high price law firm on the fifty-first floor of the 86-story MTN tower in downtown Chicago. There was a large television suspended from one corner of the ceiling. *ABC7* news was on, the volume set to low, but Markio heard the pickup truck's description loud and clear. It was the same kind of pickup Leezo drove, the same kind of pickup Markio had been on the lookout for since yesterday. He wondered if it could be the same Silverado that was just involved in a shooting on 64th and King Drive, in the infamous "O-Block" neighborhood that had birthed Chicago drill rap legends King Vaughn and Chief Keef.

Now, Leezo couldn't have been involved in that shooting. He was in Michigan City, not Chicago.

"Markio Earl? Attorney Staples will see you now"

Markio stood up and smiled, the thoughts of Leezo drifting quickly from his mind. Every seat in the waiting area was taken, and several of them had been waiting when Markio walked in ten minutes ago. Pocketing his phone, he followed this shapely young secretary down a short hallway and into a spacious office with breathtaking floor-to-ceiling views of the downtown area.

But Markio wasn't interested in what could be seen outside the windows. The honey-brown woman who rose from the white leather upholstered swivel chair behind her desk was much more breathtaking. She smiled, eyes asquint, her teeth flawlessly white as her form-fitting dress, her dark hair cut short and expertly styled.

"You," she said accusingly.

"Me, indeed." Markio sat down in one of the two comfortable leather chairs in front of her desk, his smile even wider than hers. "Long time no see, stranger."

"When did you get out of prison?"

"Last January. A few weeks before my birthday."

"I called you in here because I recognize your name. You didn't make it three minutes in middle school before you got expelled. I'll never forget that day. You sat down backwards after, desk right in front of me, and when the teacher asked you to turn around—"

"I said, 'Fuck you and this classroom. I'm trying to talk to Nikkia.' And I beat up the vice principal when I got sent to the office. I remember I got arrested that day."

Slowly, Nikkia Staples lowered herself onto the seat of her swivel chair. She gazed silently at him for a long moment, repeatedly clicking an ink pen in her hand until Markio broke the silence.

"You still look just as beautiful as you did all those years ago."

She scoffed at the compliment and held up her left hand. There was a fat diamond on her ring finger. "Boy, I am married with three kids." She lowered her hand and turned to her computer. "What do you want, Markio? I'm busy."

"I need a lawyer. A *good* lawyer. You can still practice law in Indiana, right?"

"Yes, I can. But I'm a lot more expensive than the attorneys in Michigan City. I'll need twenty grand before I even look at your case. "

Markio dug in the right hand pocket of his black Amiri jeans and struggled to pull out the huge, rubber-band piles of hundred dollar bills he'd had on him since last night. He leaned forward and pushed the cash across the desk to Nikkia, the woman he'd had a crush on ever since he first left Chicago as a kid and met her in the third grade classroom of Niemann Elementary.

She picked up the bundle of cash and studied the dime-size hole that cut about a fourth of the way through the bills. She frowned, turned the bundle over, and gave it a shake. A flattened bullet dropped out of the hole and bounced across her desk.

"What in the—?"

"I got shot last night," Markio explained. "That stack of hundreds saved my lil' leg. You should still have at least twenty thousand in there you can use. I don't care what you do with the rest."

Nikkia burst out laughing, falling back in her chair. Her laughter was soft and sweet, easy like Sunday morning. "Oh, wow. You got shot and the bullet hit this stack of cash?" She started laughing again, and Markio laughed along with her.

The light moment shattered the tension. Markio could almost feel the weight lifted out of the room, and the air became easier to breathe. Nikkia swiped her forefingers along her lower eyelids to rid them of the laughing tears threatening to slide down her gorgeous face.

"I'm sorry," she said, after she got herself under control, "but this is funny. Oh my God. I've never actually seen anything like this." She picked up her smartphone and stood to snap a photo of the flattened bullet and the wounded pile of cash. "I have to post this. Oh God, I have to post this."

"So you'll take my case?"

"Yes. Yes. Right now I don't think I have a choice." She snickered a while longer as she snapped a few more pictures. "You have to tell me what happened. Is that why you need a lawyer? Does it have anything to do with this?"

"Kinda. Well, not really. My parole officer said I need to hire a lawyer. Guess my name came up in some homicide investigations. Some nigga named G-Money got smoked yesterday, then two of his guys got killed last night, and the police think I have some to do with it. I need a good lawyer just in case they try to arrest me for that shit."

Nikkia looked at her wristwatch. Markio had already scoped in from across the desk and read the name on with the face. It was a Richard Mille, easily worth a quarter million dollars.

"How long will you be in town?" Nikkia asked.

"As long as I need to be."

"OK." She paused. "I need to get a few more clients in here before noon but if you want to meet me for lunch we can talk over your situation and see where we'll go from there. Do you know GAM's? Great Aunt Micki's? It's a five star soul food restaurant a few blocks from here. Meet me there at twelve thirty and we'll talk."

Markio nodded and stood to shake her hand, but Nikkia came around the desk and hugged him instead. He breathed in the tantalizing scent of her perfume, basking in the uniquely feminine aroma and enjoying the soft feel of her warm embrace. He pulled her tight against him and was a bit reluctant to let her go.

"It was nice seeing you," she said, pulling back, and Markio could sense that she really meant it. "I haven't seen anyone from my past in years. I can't wait to hear the story of how you ended up being saved from a bullet by a pile of cash."

"It's a date," Markio said, turning to leave.

"I didn't say a date! It's lunch!" Nikkia shouted after him, but he was already out the door, smiling harder than ever.

Markio was so happy about his "date" with the stunning attractive attorney that he failed to notice the breaking news story on the waiting area's television as he passed by on his way to the elevator.

There had been another deadly shooting involving the silver colored Chevy Silverado, this one 64th and Normal. One dead, three wounded.

Deceased victim was shot multiple times in the head.

***

Markio had purchased two cheap Nike duffel bags from Walmart and filled them with cash from one of these suitcases before giving his mother and sister the money for their trip and trailing them from Michigan City to Chicago. They had separated on the highway with Mama and Taquisha both glad to have received $8,500 each for their spur-of-the-moment vacation. They'd *FaceTimed* him shortly after he left Nikkia Staples' office, saying they had made it to O'Hare International Airport and that their flight to Aruba would be departing at 10:55 a.m.

After discovering that each rubber band bundle of cash contained approximately five hundred bills, Markio pocketed a bundle of hundreds and a bundle of fifties – $75,000 in total – then hit the Gold Coast shopping district and spoiled himself with a well deserved shopping spree.

At Louis Vuitton, he bought two duffel bags, four pairs of sneakers and numerous shirts, hats, hoodies, belts, bandanas, sunglasses, and a pair of pants and shorts. He even got himself a Louis Vuitton phone case. His bill ended up being $18,320.50, and he paid at the counter with a hundred and eighty-four $100 bills.

Afterward, he piled the bags in the back of his 2019 Mercedes-Benz GLC 300 truck and was *Googling* nearby hotels when his phone rang with a *FaceTime* call from Bankroll Reese. Pulling off from the curb in front of the Louis Vuitton, he placed his smartphone in the phone holder on his dashboard, angled the screen toward his face and answered the call.

"Multimillionaire Markio," Resse said as soon as he popped up on the screen.

Markio chuckled. "You must have talked to Bam and Worm already, huh?"

"Hell yeah. They just left not too long ago. You really got five M's off them niggas?"

"They act like I rob 'em or some'n, cuzzo. You know I don't rock like that. If I rob it ain't gon be one of the Bros. I bought that storage locker, and that mean I own everything that was in it. No exceptions. I don't care who got a problem with it."

"I'm with you, cousin," said Reese. He smiled hard, obviously intrigued by the situation. "But Worm mad as fuck right now. Watch out for that. I just warned him not to play too crazy, but that's five million. Ain't no tellin' what he gon do over that shit. I'd be mad too."

Markio gave a dismissive shrug. "I'm all on Michigan Avenue shoppin' with that nigga money. I should go live and stunt on his bitch ass. Matter of fact, I'm about to hit him and Bam on IG so I can send them my location. Fuck it."

"Nah, cousin. Don't do that. You can't front your move. That's how FBG got killed. Give one some time to cool off. I mean, do you, but just be low about it, and keep that blick on you."

"Never leave home without it," Markio said with a humorless little smirk. "I gotta hit my girl. Tell Kay and Buck I'll be through the hood to see them before I leave."

"Man, you know me, Bam and Worm gon' be over there."

"Exactly."

Markio had a .45 caliber Ruger under his seat and a Micro Draco 7.62 by 39 machine pistol and one of his cash-filled Nike duffel bags. The fire in him had been reignited yesterday afternoon, when he emerged from beside a ramshackle tool shed, wearing a ski mask and wielding a Glock handgun, and shot G-Money in the face. He hadn't wanted to go back to his old trigger-happy ways. G-Money and his gang had forced it out of him, and he couldn't wait to drop another body.

Big Worm had him fucked up.

He decided on the Four Seasons and booked the $3,800-a-night penthouse suite that came with a licensed massage therapist, five-star dining, and a bunch of other amenities. He showered and changed into a Louis summer outfit with matching sneakers, added a hat and a pair of sunglasses, then sat down to attach the new phone case to his iPhone before typing out a text to Whitney:

'*If you meet me at the Four Seasons hotel in downtown Chicago by noon I got $100K for you. I feel like I owe you that much. I wouldn't have got that locker if you hadn't taken me to that auction.*'

Markio sent the text, and less than five seconds later the message showed that it had been seen. He stared vacantly at the wavering little dots as Whitney typed a reply:

'*I'll be there in an hour. And we need to talk.*'

Markio fell back on the need, his arms outstretched like Jesus on the cross. He forced himself to ponder his chances with Nikkia, because thinking about Whitney made his heart ache. He loved

Whitney too much, and he deeply regretted breaking up with her over something so petty. But what was done was done. She wasn't making an effort to reconcile, so why should he? Whitney Clarrett was a bad bitch, but looks meant nothing without trust, and he didn't trust her.

As for Nikkia, she had made it known that she was married, and that their lunch date wasn't really a date. Something in his head kept telling him he still had a chance, and he was going to do his best to win her over, but there was a very real possibility that the lunch date would end up being all business and no pleasure.

Which brought him to his third option: the short, flawless, big-bootied redbone Mya Patterson. But she was Worm's youngest sister, and that fact alone was enough to make Markio re-evaluate their situation. She swore she'd never get involved in her brother's beefs, but five million dollars could change a person. She called him twice while he was out shopping and again when he was in the shower, and he'd ignored all three calls.

He sat up and began searching online for the nearest Mercedes dealership. Then he got up and left the suite to grab a snack and do some more shopping. Though he hated to admit it, Markio was heartbroken, but it was nothing five million dollars in drug money couldn't fix.

King Rio

Chapter Four

"We can't send the bros at the bros. You know law, nigga. That ain't how Vice Lords operate. If I bring this to the mob, everybody gone side with Markio. He bought the locker at a fuckin' auction. That's his. You need to approach this differently. Ask him for some of the money back, and apologize for sendin' Lord n'em at his girl."

Big Worm ignored Bam's advice and continued on toward the backyard storage shed behind their grandmother's home, holding a set of keys in his one good hand to unlock the shed while Bam carried three large black duffel bags that contained everything needed to mix, weigh, and package mass quantities of heroin.

1638 South Trumbull Avenue had been Bam and Worm's paternal grandmother Leila "Grammy" Patterson's home since 1956. Eighty-year-old Grammy lived in the first-floor apartment with her crackhead son Uncle Tommy. Ebony Griffin, the mother of Worm's kids, rented the second-floor apartment. And Worm rented the basement apartment from Grammy for himself. It was where he stayed when he was in the neighborhood, and also where he'd been preparing his heroin for years.

He'd had Latazia Oliver, his girlfriend, bring him his last two uncut kilos of heroin and his last kilo of Fentanyl from their modest five bedroom home in the nearby Chicago suburb of Maywood, and he and Bam had spent the last two hours mixing it all up with a cutting agent and compressing it into twelve separate one-kilogram bricks. It was by far the furthest Worm had ever stretched three kilos, but he was in a bind, and he knew the dope would still turn out good.

Bam had purchased five of the bricks for Worm's asking for $85,000 a -ki, and Chops, a Black Disciple from 64th and Normal, was buying the other seven. Latazia was en route to Englewood now to deliver the bricks and pick up the cash, and she had four cars full of Worm's sons and nephews—Worm had five adult sons, and Bam had eight—following behind her protection, each of them heavily armed and anxious to shoot.

After locking up the shed, Worm and Bam went back inside, and Worm sat at the kitchen table on his smartphone while Bam stood at the stove cooking French fries and hamburgers.

"So what you gon' do?" Bam asked, pressing especially down on a thick, sizzling beef Patty.

Worm was on Instagram, seething with anger as he scrolled down Markio's page. He double tapped a photo of Markio and Whitney sitting on a towel in the sand at some beach, just to get Markio's attention and let him know he was being watched.

"I can't ask this nigga to give me some of my money back. I just can't do it."

"Markio ain't goin' for nothing else, though. That's the thing, bruh. Dude gon whack some'n every time, period. Look at how he did that BD in Indiana. Shorty is a straight up killer. You gotta respect that."

"Respect a nigga who just took five million of my money? Nah, I ain't respect that."

"He didn't *take* shit. He bought it. Legally. If it's anybody's fault, it's that nigga who shot you, and we put him in the dirt yesterday. Lord from the same block we from."

Warm let out a low, guttery groan. Tears of frustration sprung up along his lower eyelids. As much as he hated to admit it, he knew Bam was right. He wanted his money back, but there was no way he was going to be able to convince the gang to turn on Markio. The Earl family was just as deeply ingrained in the North Lawndale community as the Patterson's. In fact, the two families were really more like one big family

"Bullshit," Worm grumbled defeatedly. "Some straight up bullshit."

"Just call him, bruh. Call Lord and holler at him man to man. What's the worst that could happen? I got his number. He sent it to me on Facebook when he got out the joint."

Worm's leg was shaking under the table; he used his forefinger to wipe away the tears. He'd taken some losses before. Just nine months ago he'd been shot in the gut and robbed of four bricks of heroin and $780,000 in cash when a dancer he met at Club Ocean had him followed from his hotel room back to his Maywood home. He had the stripper killed for making him take such a major loss, and he was supposed to just let Markio slide?

Right now he didn't seem to have much of a choice. His hand trembled as he dialed Markio's number. Part of him expected Markio not to answer, and that part of him couldn't have been more wrong. Markio answered immediately.

"Yo. Who this?"

"This Worm, man."

A thoughtful smirk crept slowly across Markio's face. He was at Mercedes-Benz of Chicago, just pulling off the lot in a brand new, matte black 2022 Mercedes-Benz S550 with the tenant windows and black Mercedes rims. He traded in his truck and put down $9,998 on the $118,000 luxury sedan, because the dealer told him they'd have to file paperwork with the IRS if he put down $10,000 or more.

The truck and back seat of his new car were crammed full of shopping bags. He'd blown another $420,000 on Michigan Avenue, buying designer gear from Givenchy, Balenciaga, Balmain, Christian Dior, Prada, Celine, and a few other high-end fashion brands, including a lambskin Chanel bag he bought for Taquisha that had cost him $3,800.

Now he was on his way back to The Four Seasons to meet up with Whitney and give her the $100,000 he promised her, and he didn't give two fucks what Worm had to say about it.

"What's the word, Lord?" Markio said, inhaling the first segment of new leather as he turned, went to the street and drove off from the dealership.

Worm took a long moment before he spoke, and when he did, his words took Markio by surprise. "I apologize, Lord. For telling Little Mark to put that pistol on you. For having a jump out on your girl like that. For having 'em break in her house. I'm man enough to admit when I'm wrong, and I was wrong. We grew up together. Had I known from jump that it was you who bought the storage locker, I would have went about this a whole nother way."

Markio's mouth dropped open in a silent, shaped chuckle. *What the fuck?* he thought, adjusting his seat. He's been ready to go to war with Worm, and now Worm was copping a plea? He didn't even consider this outcome, though in the back of his mind he knew it was what he really wanted. He didn't give a fuck about Worm, but he'd always loved Bam like a big brother, and he wasn't sure how things would turn out between him and Bam if he ended up killing Worm.

"It's cool," Markio said, and that was all. He didn't want Worm to think he was willing to return the money, because he wasn't. Not in a million years.

"You don't owe me shit, Lord," Worm continued. "Shit! You did fifteen years for a body and didn't tell nobody. You deserve a few million. I don't need you, but if you don't wanna help me get back on my feet I can't be mad at you. I just need a little something to go back to the store with. A few hundred thousand if you can stand it."

"I got you," Markio said quickly. "That's all you have to say. I'll give it to Mya and have her bring it to you. Gotta give her some money for her friend anyway."

"A'ight. Just get at me, lil' bruh. I'll be at my grandma's house building on Trumbull."

"Yep. I'll just bring it to you myself a little later," Markio said.

He cranked up the volume on Kodak Black's *Black For Everything* album and listened to smackers while he steered his shiny new chariot down Lakeshore Drive, deciding he'd murder Worm if the beef didn't end after he made the payment. He didn't fully trust Worm's proposition, but if a few hundred grand was all it took to get rid of the problem, Markio was with it. Especially if it was just $200,000 out of $5 million. He felt like he was buying his freedom, because the possibility of him violating parole or catching another murder charge already had him stressing, and he didn't want to add another homicide to the police growing list of reasons for hounding him. He'd already killed one Gangster Disciple and paid for two more killings than the last twenty-four hours alone, and he still had Leezo to deal with.

But he knew Worm and Bam sold heroin by the kilo, and would make Worm give up a few bricks for that 200,000K.

Whitney's red Honda Accord was parked across from the hotel where Markio pulled up at 11:47 A.M. There was a vacant parking space right in front of it, and she got out of her car as he eased his S550 in front of the space. He could see her in his side view mirror, dressed in a plain white T-shirt with her iKiss cosmetics logo printed across the chest and orange lettering, orange and white leggings, and a matching pair of Jordan 1. She had her hands on her hips and a genuine smile on her face as she walked around to the passenger side of his car and got in beside him.

"Wow. Didn't take you long to start splurging, huh?" Whitney looked over into the back seat and rifled through a few bags. "Givenchy. Dior. Balmain. Damn, Markio!" she said, her tone rising in amazement.

Markio was at a loss for words. Seeing Whitney up close again put in indescribable pressure on his lungs. God, she was beautiful. Her lips glistened with a hot pink gloss. Her skin glowed in the sunlight, her long black hair drawn back in two sexy braids, and Markio couldn't stop looking at her legs, loving the way the flesh of her meaty ass and thighs spread out on the tan leather seats, emphasizing her tiny waist. She was a 5'7" yellowbone with an exceptionally pretty face and a body like Instagram model Amirah Dyme, and impossibly narrow waist above, and superbly fat round ass. Markio could tell that she'd gone to certain lengths to enhance her already stunning looks, just to rub it in his face.

"Stop lookin' at me like that, Markio. And where is my money?"

"I thought you said we needed to talk?"

"Yeah. We do need to talk. We need to have a long conversation about my half of the money."

"Your half?" Markio leaned away from Whitney like Craig and Smokey did when Red took off his glasses on *Friday*. "Whoa, whoa, whoa. Wait a minute. I ain't said shit about giving you half of nothing. I paid for that locker. Now, I told you I got a hundred thousand for you. Take that and be happy."

"What's a hundred thousand to five million, Markio? Huh? Come on, now. Stop playin' with me. I had to shoot some boy in the face yesterday over that goddamn money. My kids don't even feel safe at home no more because somebody broke in my house to look for that money. You ain't about to treat me like I ain't shit 'cause you done found yourself a new little bitch to fuck on. That shit with Fat Jerm ain't no excuse, either. I fucked with that three whole years ago and now it's a problem? Stop it."

"Nah," Markio clarified, "It's a problem because you hid it from me for eighteen months when you know that was my nigga."

"OK, well, it happened. You fucked some bitches I'm friends with, too. I didn't break up with you over the ship, because it was years ago." Whitney's voice cracked a little, and her eyes became shimmery with tears. "That's so fucked up, Markio. Like on my kids, that is so fucked up. I don't even care about the money. You left me over some shit I did three years ago and moved right on to the next bitch. I had to look at you with your arms around another bitch not even five seconds before I had to kill a nigga for trying to kidnap me in front of my kids. That's just—"

She didn't get the rest out. Her words were replaced by tears sluicing down her pretty face and leaving dark streaks of eyeliner in their wake. Markio put an arm around her shoulders and pulled her into him, and she cried on his Louis Vuitton shirt.

"It wasn't five million, baby," Markio lied, rubbing his hand up and down her back. "I just got off the phone with Worm. That's who sent them niggas to your house. I squashed the whole thing, but I agreed to give him 200,000 to get back on his feet. We grew up together on Trumbull. He said it was only two million in the suitcases. Half of the suitcases was full of clothes.."

"Don't lie to me, Markio," Whitney said with a sniffle. She dug in her purse for a tissue and dabbed her face dry as she sat up straight in her seat. She blew her nose. Shook her head. "Please, don't lie."

"I ain't got no reason to lie to you. If I was gonna lie I'd just say it was all clothes and the suitcases. Three of them was full of money, and another had some more money under the clothes. That was all of it. I swear. Other than that it was all just more clothes. "

She turned to look at him, her distraught expression morphing into something bad. The corner of her top lip rose an inch, and she clenched both her hands in fists. "OK, so what happened between you and that bitch? And tell me the whole fuckin' truth."

"Didn't nothing happen. They came over with Nissa, and I hugged up on the beach because I was mad at you. That's it, I swear," he lied again.

Whitney was unconvinced. "I want you to swear to God that you didn't fuck that girl or let her suck your dick. And I already know the truth, so lie if you want to."

"I swear to God," Markio said, taking Whitney's hand in his, "I did not fuck that girl. I ain't gonna lie, she sucked my dick at the hotel last night, but I never fucked her."

Markio had some serious praying to do later on tonight.

He looked at the time on the touch screen control pad that took up half the dashboard. It was 11:52. Thirty-eight minutes until his lunch date with Nikkia Staples was due to begin. Luckily for him, GAM's was just a five-minute drive from The Four Seasons, so he had time.

"Still," Whitney said, regaining her composure, "I need more than a hundred thousand. You know how hard I've been working to get my business off the ground. And you need to get these books typed up and published. Let's get to the bag, Markio. We can make all that money legit."

"Find some typist for me. That's what we need each other for. And here," he reached for the back seat and found the bag he'd purchased for his sister. "Look what I bought for you. You've been on my mind all day."

"Mmm hmm," she hummed skeptically, taking the Chanel bag and looking it over. "Why did you have me meet you at this hotel?"

"Because I got us the penthouse suite!" Markio was impressing even himself today. He leaned in and kissed Whitney on the cheek, suddenly eager to get her into his top floor hotel room and get all that white and orange peeled off of her.

"What else did you buy me?"

"Just a purse," he said, and when Whitney gave him a cold look, he added, "Because I wanted you to be able to pick out your own clothes. Here, baby." He pulled the pile of hundreds out of his pocket and gave it to her; it was his second bundle of hundreds of the day. He'd blown through the first $50,000 on his shopping spree, as well as several more thousand and fifties. "Take that and go shopping. I got a 12:30 appointment with the lawyer I just hired. As soon as I'm done with that appointment we can go and get that Escalade you wanted. And don't worry, none of this coming out of your money. I still got that for you, okay? That sound good to you?"

Whitney nodded as she shoved the tall stack of rubber-banded cash down in her Michael Kors purse. She was trying to decide whether or not to forgive him. He could see it on her face.

Finally, after she replied to a text on her iPhone and studied her face in the front facing camera, she said, "You still got me fucked up, Markio. My sister Candace saw you all hugged up with that bitch too. You got some explaining to do, not just to Candace but to my kids, my daddy, my—"

"Okay, baby. I'll do all that, and a whole lot more."

"You better, and don't go home for a while. I drove past there after we picked up Eva from the juvenile center. You got two cops watching your house. Bush and Corely. They pat a few houses down, but it's clear who they're looking for."

"A'ight. Fuck all that, though. I'm more worried about us. We back together, or what?"

"Mhm. We good." She said it noncommittally; there was still some thinly-veiled attitude there, probably because Markio had just confessed to getting his dick sucked by another woman, but he could deal with that. "Oh, and I know you shot G-Money after him and his boys jumped my son. Whether you admit it or not, I know it was you. So thanks."

She pushed open her door and started to climb out of the car, but Markio took hold of her waist and pulled her back in. She narrowed her eyes at him.

"I can't get no kiss?" he asked pleadingly.

"Nope." Whitney snatched her waist from his grasp, but she remained seated. "Just like that last Jordan Peele movie. Go get a kiss from that bitch. "

Markio chuckled at her sexy attitude. "Baby, I really did get us a penthouse suite. Let me get you situated in there before I go. You can get a full body massage, order whatever you want to eat, and relax until I get back from the appointment."

"Good. I need to use the bathroom anyway."

They got out of the car and without saying another word until they were inside the hotel, crossing the vast marble floor to the elevators. And even then she only said, "Unblock me on Facebook before I have to bust your goddamn head in front of all these white people."

Markio showed all his teeth in an embarrassed smile. He'd forgotten all about blocking her. He quickly did the *unblock* and sent Whitney a friend request as they were entering the elevator, and he spent the ride up to the top floor gazing wantonly at her ass while she stared straight ahead at the reflective steel doors with her arms folded across her chest.

By the time they reached the penthouse suite, his dick was hard as a flagpole. He glanced at his rose gold Rolex watch for the time: 12:06 p.m.

Shit, he thought, clenching his teeth and sighing through his nose. If not for the warning from his parole officer, he'd have skipped the meeting with Nikkia Staples altogether. But he needed a lawyer. The police in Michigan City were itching to arrest him, and one arrest could mean a parole violation, sending him back into the hellish prejudiced Indiana prison system.

Reluctantly, he returned to the elevator, preparing himself for the lunch date that wasn't really a date.

Chapter Five

There was a meeting scheduled for 12:30 P.M. at the Michigan City Police Department headquarters. Chief Martin Swiztek was already seated at the head of the long wooden table when nine more policemen and four ATF agents joined him inside conference room A.

Swizz leaned back in his swivel chair, rotating from left to right with his pale white fingers interlaced on the stomach of his magenta colored button-up shirt. The department he oversaw was usually filled with smiling faces—minus the perpetually grumpy Officer Calloway—but there wasn't a smile in the bunch this afternoon, and for good reason.

With three homicides in the last twenty-four hours and another that had been ruled justifiable, the entire department was on edge. Mayor Mitch Dumbkowski was already breathing down Swizz's neck; the republican mayor wanted more arrests, and Swizz was going to get it.

When everyone was seated, Lieutenant Darren Corley, the only black policeman in the room, got up and aimed a remote at the wall-mounted 70-inch computer monitor. A mug shot of a light-complexioned black man with two teardrops inked below his left eye appeared on the screen. Corley allowed a moment for everyone to view the mug shot before he addressed the room.

"The man we're all looking at is Makio Earl, our only suspect in yesterday's murder of Gregory "G-Money" Samuels. Germaine McCoy, one of the victims in last night's double homicide, had just called Detective Ricks with information on the Samuels murder, saying his friend, Dennis Carter, had seen the shooter standing over G-Money's body with the gun in his hand. He had a mask, but apparently he looks like Markio to Carter. And not even twenty minutes after Jermaine McCoy made the call to Ricks, Carter and McCoy were gunned down on 6th and Cedar Streets."

"Do we have a motive?" asked Detective Nicolette Mulberry, a lanky blonde with seven years on the force.

"We do," said Corely. "It's not enough to charge him, but it certainly establishes a clear-cut motive. We received a video this morning from a concerned Facebook user who believes the attack we're about to watch may be tied to yesterday's shooting."

He pressed the button on the remote, and a video began to play. It showed a young black man being kicked and punched by four older black men in the middle of a parking lot. Corley paused with the video on each of the older men's faces to highlight their identities. Gregory "G-Money" Samuels, Dennis Carter, Jermaine McCoy, and a fourth man who was brown-skinned and slender with long dreadlocks. When the video ended, the victim of the assault lay unconscious and bleeding on the asphalt while Jermaine McCoy removed the Jordans from his feet.

"The boy who was assaulted is Whitney Clarrett's seventeen-year-old son, James Thomas Jr." Corley pressed the button, and the video was replaced by a mugshot of Whitney Clarrett. "And yes, I do mean the same Whitney Clarrett who pulled the trigger in our justifiable homicide case yesterday. She's Markio Earl's girlfriend—Well, one of his girlfriends. Mya Patterson, the girl who shot the guy at the Marriott last night, said he was her boyfriend, too."

Officer Pete Caldwell, a seventeen-year police veteran who served in the Navy before becoming a beat cop, said, "So Markio Earl's stepson was jumped on by these four guys. He responds by killing G-Money and maybe even killing McCoy and Carter later in the day."

"Yes and no," said Corley. "Markio could have done the first killing, but he was at the Marriott Hotel when Carter and McCoy were killed."

"So what do we have on them?" said Swiztek, the sharpness in his tone betrayed his writhing frustration with the case.

"Not much," said Corley. "We know he's killed before. He served fifteen years for shooting a guy fourteen times at point-blank range. And yesterday his girlfriend justifiably killed a man for the second time in three years. She shot and killed Jarvell Holmes, the father of her twin daughters, in October of '19."

"Markio Earl," Swizz cut in, removing his tortoise frame glasses and pinching the bridge of his nose. "He's the key here. What can you tell us about him?"

"Well, I can tell you this: there's no sense in trying to bring him in without an arrest warrant. He won't talk. He'll lawyer up before we even get him in custody. Our eyewitness to G-Money's murder is dead, and no one saw who killed him but we know it wasn't Markio. The most we can do at this time is pull him over and hopefully catch him with something that'll violate his parole."

"What kind of vehicle does he drive?" one ATF agent asked.

"A white Mercedes-Benz GLE 300," answered Swizz. "Corley will send you all the license plate number. I want every officer in this department looking for that truck, and when you pull it over, I want it searched from top to bottom. I already have two plain-clothes officers watching his house on Vail Street, and I want that house searched too. He's a parolee, and he is a serious violent felon. That gives us the right to search his home and vehicle whenever we suspect him for being involved in a crime."

"We'll get him," said the ATF agent. "He's a Chicago gang member. These guys never stop doing crime. I'd bet my mortgage that we have him arrested by the weekend, and if we catch him with a gun he'll spend the rest of his miserable life in a federal prison."

Swizz didn't feel that same confidence. "Mulberry," he said, standing up, "I want you to contact a few of our best informants and set them loose on Markio Earl. See what they can get out of him. If he's dealing, set up a buy. I want this guy off the streets."

"Will do," said Detective Mulherry, already texting on her department-issued smartphone.

Chapter Six

GAM's was the first restaurant Markio had ever visited that had a special room in the back exclusively for its VIP customers. It was called the Red Room, and a pretty young female waitress with a Jamaican accent led Markio straight to it, where Nikkia sat looking at a digital menu on an iPad and bobbing her head to the soulful tunes of a Beyoncé song that was drifting down from speakers hidden somewhere in the high ceiling.

Markio sat down and smiled at the beautiful lawyer. "Let me guess," he said. "That drop-top Bentley parked out front—it's yours, ain't it?"

Nikkia nodded without looking up from the menu. "A gift from Alexus Castilla."

"Get the fuck outta here," Markio said skeptically. Alexus Castilla was worth hundreds of billions of dollars. She was the CEO of Castilla Corp., which owned the minority television network and all the hugely successful reality shows it produced, among other businesses. Alexus was also married to Blake "Bullet Face" King, the wealthiest rap artist alive. "You really know Alexus?"

"Why do you think my offices are located inside the MTN Tower?"

"I don't know. I didn't think about that."

Nikkia looked up from the iPad and regarded him with a close-mouthed smile. She studied his Louis Vuitton attire, leaning to the side to see his shorts and shoes. "You're cute or whatever. You may not be all that bright, but you're definitely cute. "

"What!" Markio chuckled merrily. "Yeah, you got me all the way fucked up. On gang I'm brilliant. Like a five-pointed star in the sky."

"Oh, my God," she said, her perfect white squares of teeth making an appearance in the smile. "You remind me of Bulletface."

Markio took that as a compliment. He picked up the second computer tablet, suddenly realizing that the thick-mustached bald man seated at the next table was none other than *Family Feud* host Steve Harvey, and his lunch date was his gorgeous daughter, Lori

Harvey. Markio didn't recognize any of the people seated at the other eight tables, but they all looked rich. Four waiters stood nearby with their backs to the wall and towels draped over their forearms, like the house slaves in the movie *Django Unchained*.

Markio ordered a twelve-ounce steak, mashed potatoes with gravy, sweet corn, and lemonade to drink. He had no idea what Nikkia ordered, because they placed their orders on the iPads. He set his down and took out his phone to check his notifications while Nikkia finished ordering her lunch.

He saw that Mya had just sent him a text message: '*Lil' Mark just died. That means I killed somebody to protect you, and you won't even answer my calls.*'

"Oh shit," he mouthed silently, and replied: '*I'll call you in about 30. Meeting w/ a lawyer.*'

His nephew, Tyquan, to whom he had given his last fourteen pounds of gelato to sell before he left for Chicago this morning, had texted him, too: '*Unc, Looch paid for the whole bow up front. What you want me to do with this 15k? Can I get $500?*'

'*Keep the whole $15k. The other 13 bows yours too. Look out for your brothers. Love you, nephew,*' Markio replied, his chest swelling with pride as he pictured the smile on his nephew's face.

He pocketed his phone just as Nikkia placed her tablet on the table. They looked into each other's eyes for a long moment, neither of them speaking–not with their mouths, at least.

Nikkia had put on a diamond necklace, but aside from that she looked exactly as she had in her office. No. There was something else different about her appearance, something that made Markio's eyes go wide and his hopes rise through the roof. The ring she'd had on her finger was gone.

"So," she said finally, "tell me how you ended up catching a bullet in the cash." She snickered at the play on words, and Markio gave her the stale face.

"That was too lame," he said.

"Whatever. It was funny to me." She moved her hands off the table, perhaps hoping Markio hadn't noticed her missing ring. "So what happened? What charges should I be expecting to defend you against? Start from the beginning, and don't leave anything out."

"Three people got killed in Michigan City yesterday. One in the afternoon, two more last night. I was at the crib when the first murder happened, and I was at the Marriott when that double murder went down. People think I did it because they had just jumped, uh—one of my lil' guys. My ex's son. Anyway, my parole officer said it would be in my best interest to hire an attorney. I heard you were the best in the game."

It was Nikkia's turn to put on the stale face. "Okay. All that sounds very convincing. Now, tell me what really happened."

"That's it. I just told you everything."

"I need to know it all, Markio. So they can't hit me with any surprises. Hotels have cameras. Were you really there last night or not?"

"On my cousin Joseph's grave, I was at the Marriott Hotel when that double murder went down on 6th and Cedar. The cops even know that. Some niggas tried to rob me and my lil' buddy in the elevator. The nigga who had the gun on me shot me in the leg as he went down, and the bullet hit the cash I had in my pocket."

"What about the other murder? Is there a possibility that a camera might've captured you somewhere in the vicinity?"

Markio said nothing. He only stuck out his lower lip and looked at her.

"Okay," she said, after a while. "That silence tells me everything I need to know and prepare for. I looked into your parole officer, too. She's a nice sista from South Bend, cares a lot for her parolees. She's gone to some BLM events, which means she has a soft spot for guys like you. Keep her in your corner. She'll probably give you information the police don't want you to know."

"Yeah, she looks out for me. Always warns me a week before my piss tests."

"You got a gun on you?"

Markio went silent again.

"Oh Jesus, please don't tell me it's the weapon you—"

"No, no, no. Not at all. That's gone."

Nikkia breathed a sigh of relief. "Still, you shouldn't be armed. I mean, I understand you having one on you here in Chicago, but when you cross back over into Indiana, have someone else hold it for you. Possessing a firearm is legal for everyone over eighteen in Indiana now, as long they don't have a felony. If you have enough cash on you to stop a bullet, I'm sure you have enough cash to pay someone to be your armed security. If the police have you listed as a suspect in an unsolved homicide, they'll be pulling you ever to search your car for the murder weapon. You're on parole, so they can legally search you, your vehicle, and your residence without the need of a search warrant, "

"I just bought a new car not even an hour ago," Markio said as the Jamaican waitress arrived to deliver their meals and pick up the iPads. "But I'll have somebody around me who can legally carry. You're right. Thanks."

As they began to eat—Nikkia had ordered steak and lobster with a side of yellow rice and water—Markio contemplated his relationship with Whitney and tried to decide if it was worth saving. He'd never cheated on her until he linked with Mya yesterday, and that was only after he'd learned that Whitney and his close friend— Fat Jerm—had been hiding the fact that they had fucked around a few years back. If Whitney would keep that from him, what else would she hide? He loved her to death, and he really did miss her company, but he felt the trust he'd had in her was irreparably broken. He was already questioning what she was up to while he was here with Nikkia, and he didn't want to end up being the type of man who checked his woman's phone for signs of cheating every time she walked in the door.

Fuck it, he thought, looking up from his steak to study the high-class woman seated across from him. He'd go all in with Nikkia, if he could, because as much as he loved Whitney, he knew deep down that their relationship was essentially over.

"I have never in my life sat across from a woman as beautiful as you are," he said, and he watched Nikkia's pretty face light up with happiness as she chewed.

She raised a hand to cover her mouth. "Thank you," she said.

"Ain't no need to thank me for the truth."

Nikkia rolled her eyes, beaming, and they went on eating for a few more minutes, until Markio finally got up the courage to address the elephant in the room.

"What happened to your ring?"

Nikkia took a long time to answer. She wiped her mouth with a napkin. Held out her hand and looked at the naked ring finger, as if the huge rock she'd worn earlier was still there.

"I got divorced last year," she said. "I only wear the ring to keep the bugaboos away."

"Aww, shit!" Markio's hopes continued on beyond the roof, ascending to the heavens.

"So you took off the ring for me! Don't worry, I'll put an even bigger ring on that finger."

Her eyes rolled up in their sockets again, and they fell into an easy-flowing conversation that lasted another thirty minutes. She told him about her three sons and all the sports they were involved in, and about the half-sister she'd been thinking about making up with. He told her some of the most memorable stories from his fifteen-year prison stint, from the time a so-called street nigga named Lebaron James got caught getting Skittles eaten out of his ass by a 6'7" homosexual, to the time he'd stabbed himself in the hand with a shank while stabbing a Gangster Disciple called Shorty G for breaking his cell phone and refusing to pay for a new one.

"Yep," Nikkia concluded. "You're so much like Blake. Wait until I tell Alexus about this."

"Be more than a one-time thing, right? Or am I wrong?" Markio asked hopefully.

Nikkia answered by taking out her iPhone and asking him for his phone number. "I'm not supposed to be dating my clients," she said, "so you'd better be nice. One slip-up and I'll blow the case on purpose."

Markio laughed heartily. As far as he was concerned, the "lunch" date was a success.

He'd won over his childhood crush with honesty. Now all he needed to do was seal the deal.

"I know I can get a kiss before we leave," he said, not hopefully, but prayerfully.

She put down her phone, narrowed her sexy brown eyes, and spread her lips in another close-mouthed smile. Then she leaned forward over her plate, and he leaned forward over his, and their lips met over the center of the table. Her lips were softer than cotton. Markio kissed them passionately, repeatedly, until she pulled back and unleashed a muted sigh of sexual frustration.

"Where are you staying?" she asked.

"I got a suite at the Four Seasons. "

"Good. I'll be coming by there when I'm done with work later this afternoon. I've got a court appearance for one of Derrick Rose's cousins and a plea hearing for that billionaire real estate investor who killed his wife last year, but I'll be free after that. And you'd better have protection and be ready to do some grown-up activities. Don't judge me, either. It's been a while, and I need it."

"No judgement here." Markio grinned suggestively.

"I bet there isn't." She opened her oversized Chanel purse and fished two hundred dollar bills.

Markio held up a hand to stop her.

"I got it. This one on me," he said.

"I know," she replied. This is your money. By the way, you had $35,400 in hundreds that were still usable. The rest were destroyed, but I still have them in my drawer at the office. You can have those back if you want them, but I'm keeping the good ones."

Standing up and licking his lips to taste the remaining vestiges of lobster juice she'd left there, Markio offered up no objections. He couldn't remember a time in recent history when he'd felt more optimistic and alive as he walked Nikkia out to her snow-white Bentley GT convertible and then crossed the street to get in his Benz.

Nikkia took a moment to look out her car window and admire his sleek new S550. Then she nodded approvingly and pulled off from the curb, and Markio did the same, only he was nodding in agreement with the trajectory of his day.

The beef with Worm was essentially over, leaving Markio with only Leezo to deal with. He'd briefly considered bringing his cousins Kay and Buck back to Michigan City with him, so he could have a few more shooters on hand, but that was when he and Worm were still at odds. He didn't need them now. He could handle Leezo himself.

Once he got back to his penthouse suite, he'd call Sway and Shannon Swanson to see if they'd located Leezo yet. He'd already paid them $10,000 up front to get rid of Leezo, and he'd promised them another $10,000 once the job was done. And after speaking with the Swanson brothers, Markio planned to bless Whitney with another pile of cash and send her on her way for good, perhaps after talking her into sucking him off one last time.

Markio had money now. He was, in Bankroll Reese's words, 'Multimillionaire Markio'. If he could pay to have his enemies taken care of while he laid up in a penthouse suite with a sexy-ass lawyer like Nikkia Staples, then that's what he would do.

And getting Leezo killed from sixty miles away would be a piece of cake, he thought, pressing *play* on the Kodak Black's album as he drove to the Four Seasons.

Markio Earl couldn't have been more wrong.

Chapter Seven

Markio's twenty-six-year-old nephew Tyquan had never in his life had $5,000 until today, and he wanted everyone to see it. He held the stack of cash up to his ear and recorded a selfie video for Snapchat.

"You see it, bitch!" he said, sneak-dissing his ex-girlfriend, Porsha, who watched his every move on Snap. Angry that he hadn't bought her a gift for her birthday last month, she'd left him for Kema, a grimey young jackboy from Hammond, Indiana, and Tyquan had been dissing the couple on social media ever since. "I bet your broke-ass boyfriend ain't got two dollars to his name. I got racks over here, bitch. You see it. This ain't shit but a light five jeez. Plenty more where this came from. Bitch, I got bows of gelato for the low. One-day sale. Four racks apiece. Come and get 'em if you got it."

He blew a cloud of weed smoke at the camera and ended the video. He was sitting in his eight-year-old Nissan Sentra, with an unattractive light-skinned girl named Merlyn in the seat beside him. His equally unemployed friends—Roaster and Benji—were in the backseat; Benji with a. 25-caliber Smith & Wesson pistol on his lap. The gun had brown tape wrapped around the handle and nine rounds in the clip. Roaster didn't have a weapon at all.

They were parked in the rear of Coolspring Apartments, just outside the building where Merlyn and her young daughter lived in her sparsely furnished one-bedroom apartment. Tyquan had a gun, too: a 9-millimeter Mac-11 with a 30-round clip. He had it tucked off in his door panel, in close reach.

Looking at his phone, Tyquan smiled triumphantly. The views on his video were already going up. Porsha had seen it. Laura, a brown-skinned girl who lived toward the front of the apartment complex, had also seen the video, as well as her friend—Democon. In fact, two hundred and four people—mostly boys and girls in their late teens and early twenties who'd been tuned in to the beef for weeks now— had viewed the video within the first minute of it being posted.

"That nigga Kema a lame, bro," Roaster said, reaching one fat arm between the seats to grab the blunt from Merlyn. "I was in boy's school with that nigga. He got beat up by a whole white boy. Swear to God. And he ain't wanna do shit about it. White boy mopped him all through the chow hall."

"He just went live on Facebook," said Benji. He was a dark-skinned, seventeen-year-old pretty boy, dressed in a Reebok T-shirt and black denim shorts over black Reebok Classics. He and his older cousin—Flocka—had moved up from Evansville with Benji's alcoholic sister a few years ago, and he'd quickly become popular with all the high school girls.

Kema had blocked Tyquan on Facebook, so he watched Kema's profanity-filled rant on Benji's smartphone:

"Macan, this bitch ass nigga Tyquan done came up on a few racks and now this pussy think he on some'n. You ain't on shit, lil' nigga. You out here tryna live off your uncle's name. Yo uncle might be a killa and all that, and he doin' his thong with the bows, got a Benz truck, and a badass bitch, but nigga, what you got? You ain't got shit, lil' nigga! You ain't even got no bitch! I took yo bitch, you lil' bum-ass nigga. Ridin' around in that dirty-ass Nissan—"

Tyquan laughed to keep from crying. "This nigga a straight bitch. He ain't gon' say that—"

His words ceased at the sound of screeching tires. He looked in his rearview mirror and saw that two vehicles had just swooped in behind him, blocking him in.

A silver Chevy pickup truck and a black Buick Regal.

Benji and Roaster turned in their seats to look out the back window as the doors on both vehicles flew open. The driver and two passengers in the pickup jumped out wearing ski-masks and aiming guns at Tyquan's car. Two more masked gunmen got out of the Buick. A few of them had assault rifles.

Tyquan gasped and raised his hands in surrender. Benji pushed the small-caliber pistol off his lap and raised his hands, too. Roaster's fat brown hands (the fingernails still stained red from the large bag of *Flamin' Hot Cheetos* he'd eaten less than an hour ago) were the last to go in the air. Merlyn's hands only came up to cover her mouth and mute the scream that came out of her as the barrel of an AR-15 came in through her open window and poked her in the face.

"Man, I hope you didn't just get us killed, " Benji said shakily.

The gunmen snatched open all four doors of Tyquan's dusty old Sentra and ordered everyone out at gunpoint. The one at Tyquan's door—the man who'd driven the pickup—grabbed the cash out of Tyquan's hand, then took the Mac. 11 from the door panel and stuck it down in his pants.

"Which one of y'all Markio's nephew?" he asked.

Lying face-down on the asphalt, Roaster pointed a chubby forefinger at Tyquan, and the man who'd taken Tyquan's money raised his mask to show Tyquan who he was. Tyquan had just gotten down to his knees outside his open car door, and he looked up at the face of a man he'd seen several times over the past couple of months. He couldn't remember his name, but he knew the man was from Chicago, and that he was a GD.

"Remember this face. I'm Leezo G. Tell your uncle I said stop hidin' and come outside before I kill you," the man said, smacking the pile of cash on Tyquan's forehead.

Then he and his fellow gunmen turned and ran back to their vehicles. Tyquan didn't realize he'd pissed in his sweatpants until he looked up and saw the stunned faces of four black women who were standing about twenty feet up the sidewalk, in front of someone else's apartment door. He quickly lowered his eyes, too embarrassed and humiliated by the incident to look the women in the eye, and he saw the pool of urine spreading out around his knees.

Tyquan stood up as soon as the gunmen sped off, and climbed back into his car, heart pounding, hands shaking. Nobody else joined him in the car, so he backed out and drove off by himself.

***

When Leezo and his Tackaville gang first walked into Laura's apartment, neither of them had been expected to be leaving right back out in less than two minutes.

Shortly after he moved to Michigan City, Leezo and Laura's friend, Democon, had met at Mugshots, a local karaoke bar, and they'd been sneaking and linking ever since. Leezo had called a few of his hoes during the drive from Chicago, and Democon was the only one who picked up, inviting him and the gang to hang out at Laura's apartment. When Laura's sister—Alycia—opened the doors and let them in, Democon and Laura were sitting in the living room, watching a Snapchat video on Democon's smartphone.

"This nigga Tyquan is cappin' so hard right now," Democon was saying. "I ain't never seen him with no money before this video. You know he got that shit from Markio."

Leezo had been staring at Alycia's ass as she walked into the living room when his attention flashed over to Democon.

"Who you say?" he asked.

"Tyquan. This boy beefin' with Kema over a—"

"Nah, the other name. You said Markio?"

"Mm-hmm. Crazy-ass Markio. He from Chicago, too. He been laid back since he got out the joint, but that boy used to terrorize these niggas out here."

"Where he live at?"

All three of the black women had turned to look at Leezo. Neither of them spoke, but the apprehension in their eyes spoke volumes.

"Where he live at?" Leezo had repeated, more sternly that time.

"I don't know where Markio stays, but his nephew fucks with Merlyn, the lil' light-skinned girl who stays in the back of these apartments. That's where he's at now. Look, he just posted this video on Snap."

That was how Leezo, Wooski, Tutu, Fat Head, Jay Loud, and Ikey had known where to find Markio's nephew.

"We should've smoked that lil' nigga," Wooski said. He was in the passenger's seat beside Leezo, rolling his ski-mask to his forehead. "On fo'nem. We should've rolled him up."

"Nah," Leezo said, shaking his head as he steered his Silverado out of the apartment complex.

"We ain't in Chiraq. You gotta move different out here. They had four murders out here yesterday. That might be normal at the crib, but it set this lil' city on fire. We just gon' catch that nigga who killed Folks n'em. Then we back in the 'Raq"

"Fuck that, G. I'm tryna whack same'n."

"You wanna whack some'n every day. Ever since Folks got whacked last month, you been on a killin' spree."

The "Folks" who was whacked last month was FBG Cash, shot and killed on June 10th while sitting in his car with a hood girl who was also shot. Wooski and the rest of the gang off St. Lawrence had been sliding on opps ever since, trying their best to catch any and every 300 BD lacking so they could put them up there with Cash and Duck.

Leezo's phone lay on his lap, next to the Mac-11 he'd taken from Markio's nephew. He felt it buzz on his crotch and picked it up to read the new text message. It was from Democon:

'Markio lives somewhere on Vail Street. I asked my homegirl Nissa where I could find him so I could buy some loud and she said he just moved into a house on Vail. It's right up the block from where that boy got killed trying to kidnap Whitney Clarrett yesterday. Waiting on her to send me the exact address now, but you should see his white Benz truck out there'.

Leezo smiled wickedly. "See?" He showed Wooski the text. "Trust me on this. I know how to move out here, Folks."

From the backseat, Lil' Jay said, "What? We got action?"

Leezo nodded, "Yup. I just got the drop on that fuck nigga. We on his ass."

***

"I'm tellin' you, Whitney. The cops is still watchin' this house. I can't just break in when they're sittin' right there on front street."

Yes, you can, Flocka. You can kick in the back door and go in that way. They're not watching the back of the house."

"You sure you can pay me fifty thousand dollars for doin' this?"

"I'm absolutely sure. Look at this." Whitney held up a huge, rubber-banded pile of hundred-dollar bills for Flocka to see. "This fifty thousand right here. Markio just gave it to me. If you can give me those eight suitcases, me and you can move away and get married. I promise."

Flocka showed a cheesy smile. "And I'ma eat that ass every day," he said, lowering his voice to a seductive whisper. "For breakfast, lunch, and dinner. "

"Boy, you are so nasty." Whitney laughed, and her tongue came out between her teeth before she added, "Just get in there and get those suitcases. And hurry up."

Flocka blew a loud, smacky kiss at Whitney, and she ended the *FaceTime* call.

Pocketing his phone, he looked over at Mellie Mel, who sat behind the wheel of the beat-up old gray minivan.

"So," Mellie Mel asked, "she really got fifty racks for us to do this shit?"

"She got fifty racks for *me* to do this shit, "Flocka corrected. "I'll break bread with you for me over here, but that's my money. She don't even know you with me."

"Nah, fuck that. Fuck that. I want half."

"Keep talkin', you ain't go-getter shit, nigga."

Mellie Mel chuckled and puffed on his Black & Mild cigar. "I can't believe you actually fucked Whitney Clarrett. I wouldn't even know what to do with all that ass. That bitch so fuckin' bad. I ain't gon' lie, I would've ate that ass, too. You wrong for fuckin' Lil' Jimmy's mama, though. That's our nigga."

"Like you wouldn't do it if she gave you a chance."

"You think she would?" Mellie Mel asked, his voice full of hope.

Flocka shrugged his broad shoulders. "I'll try to talk her into it. Let's try to get these suitcases first. Pull into that alley over there."

Mellie Mel keyed the ignition, and the rickety old engine coughed to life. As they pulled from the curb and crossed the street to enter the alleyway that ran alongside Markio's house, Flocka looked at the two cops sitting in a parked blue Ford Explorer a few houses down. The cops were laughing about something, looking at each other, not paying the rust-laden minivan any attention.

Flocka was a grimey young nigga who'd do just about anything for some money, as long as it didn't go against the code of the streets. The whole reason he'd moved to Michigan City with his cousins Dreka and Benji to begin with was because he'd robbed a small bank in Evansville for $37,000, and during the robbery he'd accidentally shot a security guard in the neck, leading the FBI to offer a $75,000 reward for information leading to an arrest. Dreka had offered to get him out of the city as long as he gave her $5,000 to get them an apartment and some furniture, and he'd quickly taken her up on the offer, even going as far as helping Dreka buy a car for work (which she'd totaled in a drunk driving crash back in April) and helping her get another car to drive for Lyft (which Dreka had wrecked in a second DUI incident that led to the loss of her license and sixty days in jail).

The bank money was all gone now, and $50,000 was just what Flocka needed to get back on his feet, because his job at the local bakery wasn't cutting it.

He had Mellie Mel park alongside Markio's fenced-in backyard. They got out and stood together for a moment, looking around, the hoods of their sweaters drawn tight around their heads.

"Hot as hell out here, and we got on hoodies," Mellie Mel complained bitterly.

Flocka waved off the complaint. He went to the chain-link fence, unlatched the gate, and looked around one last time. The only potential eyewitness he saw was the driver of a silver pickup truck driving past on Vail; the driver, a brown-hued black man with dreads, seemed to look right at Flocka as his pickup passed the mouth of the alley and continued on down the street, but Flocka kept his cool, opening the gate and walking up on to the back porch as if he owned the place. Looking back into the yard, he noticed a section of the fence was missing, and there were tire tracks in the grass.

"Was that pussy wet as fuck?" Mellie Mel asked. He was about 5'6" and a bit on the heavy side, with an acne-scarred face and the worst sense of style Flocka had ever seen.

Flocka tried turning the doorknob. It was locked. "Hell yeah. Wet as fuck, on the G. I sucked the juice out that pussy, too."

"Damn," Mellie Mel said, moving aside as Flocka prepared to kick the door. "She got badass daughters, too. I wanna fuck Eva and Ava so bad. Two sexy-ass twins, with fat asses and nice-ass titties— that's the kinda shit niggas like us can only dream about. I know they only sixteen but I'll fuck both of them bad bitches. With no regrets, on my mama. I don't care they can arrest me for that shit anyway. I'm only three years older than them."

"Man, shut the fuck up."

Flocka ran at the door and kicked just above the doorknob, and the door flew right open, splintering wood all over the floor inside the doorway, which opened into a small kitchen. He quickly moved inside, ready to turn and haul ass if he heard an alarm go off. But there was no alarm. Mellie Mel stepped inside and allowed the door shut behind them, his beady eyes darting around.

"Did she say where to look?" Mellie Mel, checking the pantry.

"Yeah. The master bedroom. She said it should be eight steel suitcases in there, but he might've moved 'em to another room."

They crept through the kitchen, then through the dining room, then around a corner through the living room and finally into a short hallway with three open doors.

The door on the right was clearly the bedroom Whitney had described. She'd told him there'd be a brown fur Louis Vuitton blanket on the bed, and sure enough there it was, draped over a bed that looked large enough to sleep four adults.

But there weren't any suitcases standing up next to the bed, as Whitney had suggested there might be. Flocka balled his large hands into fists and clenched his teeth tightly together.

"I don't see no suitcases," Mellie Mel said.

"No shit." Flocka walked around the bed. Lifted the mattress. Looked in the closet.

No suitcases.

"Let's check the other rooms," he said, turning to leave the bedroom.

The other two doors in the hallway led into the bathroom and a linen closet, so they went back out to the living room and started up the stairs to the second floor.

"I don't see. Whitney ain't tried to give me that pussy," Mellie Mel pondered aloud. "I'm short and light-skinned just like that nigga Markio."

"Yeah, but you ain't nothin' like him. He get money, and he ain't no lame."

"I ain't no lame, nigga. I just ain't got no hustle. I can't hustle to save my life. You know how many niggas I done had put me on? I blow that shit every time. Loochie gave me a QP one time and I smoked all that shit in like two weeks. My daddy gave me two hundred Percocets, and I sold every pill and blew all the money on my baby mama Dejané. Now I'm hearin' the baby she pregnant with ain't even mine. My pops told me this mornin' he think it's his baby."

Flocka was quickly growing tired of hearing Mellie Mel talk.

When they made it upstairs they found all the rooms completely empty. There was a padlock on one bedroom door, but it was open, and there was nothing in the room except for an ashtray with a single cigarette butt in it, nesting on the window sill next to a dead fly.

"Welp," said Mellie Mel. "There went that fifty racks."

"Shut—the fuck—up." The words came out of Flocka in guttural growl.

Flocka's phone began to vibrate in his pocket, and as he took it out he told Mellie Mel to go and check the basement. Mellie Mel drew his pistol, a 38-caliber revolver with a black rubber grip, and took the stairs two at a time on the way back down to the first floor

Seeing Mellie Mel with his gun out reminded Flocka that he was in a real-life gangsta's house. Whitney had assured him that Markio was in Chicago with her, but he figured he could never be too careful, so he pulled out his own pistol, a 40-caliber semiautomatic Springfield.

The phone call wasn't from Whitney, as he'd expected. It was his cousin Benji. He stuck one AirPod in his ear and answered the call.

"Man, I just got robbed," Benji said. Some niggas just jumped out on us wit' choppas and pistols. We was sittin' in the car wit' Tyquan dumb ass, and some niggas pulled up on us outta nowhere. They was wearin' ski-masks. One nigga had a Draco, another one had a AR."

"You good? They didn't touch you, did they?" Flocka asked as he started off down the stairs, moving even faster than Mellie Mel had a moment earlier.

"Nah, nah, I'm good. The nigga who had the gun on me just took the money and the roxies I had in my pocket. It was really about Tyquan's uncle. The nigga who robbed Tyquan pulled up his mask and said some'n like, *'Tell Markio it's Leezo, stop hidin' from me.'* That's what Roaster say he heard. I was on the other side of the car."

"Where was y'all at when this happened?"

"In Coolspring. You know Merlyn, the ugly lil' lightskin girl who stay a few doors down from us? We was parked in front of her spot. The niggas pulled up behind us in a black car and a gray pickup truck, hopped out with all kinda guns. Shit was crazy. I thought we was dead."

An image of the silver pickup truck Flocka had seen driving past on Vail a few minutes flashed in his mind. In the living room, he stopped to look out the vertical blinds. No sign of the pickup, but he was still a little concerned.

"You said a gray pickup?" he asked worriedly.

"Yeah. Like a silver-gray. Man, you should've seen Tyquan. That nigga pissed on hisself. He had just sold a pound of weed to a nigga for five racks, and he got the whole five racks snatched right out his hand. The nigga took his Mac-11, too. I got to keep my gun. It had pushed off my lap to the floor when they hopped out on us, and I reached back in there and grabbed it when they ran off." Benji laughed, but Flocka wasn't in a laughing mood.

He moved on into the kitchen and looked down the basement steps as Mellie Mel came jogging back up them, still clutching his pistol.

"Ain't shit down there but a bed and some couches, a few TVs," Mellie Mel said. "Let's get outta here."

Flocka told Benji he'd hit him back and hung up. Mellie Mel used the sleeve of his hooded sweatshirt to open the back door, tucking the Smith & Wesson .38 in the back waistline of his jeans.

Flocka was reluctant to conceal his weapon. He wanted to see out into the alleyway first. Make sure that silver pickup wasn't out there. There was an ominous feeling in his stomach, a primal instinct that was telling him to keep his gun in his hand. Just in case he needed it.

His instincts had never let him down before, and they didn't let him down this time, either.

Mellie Mel had only stepped one foot outside the door when Flocka saw the short barrel of Draco pistol appear from the right side of the doorway, aimed at the side of Mellie Mel's head.

Flocka's eyes and mouth went wide with fear. He reached out to grab the back of Mellie Mel's hoodie, but fire burst forth from the Draco's barrel before his fingertips could touch the fabric, and Mellie Mel's head rocked sharply to the left, leaning into an explosion of meaty red brain stew that splashed violently out of his skull.

Flocka stumbled backward, knocking over a chair and raising his pistol just as the short dark-skinned boy holding the Draco stepped into the doorway. Flocka began squeezing the trigger, striking him low in the abdomen with the first shot and through the right shoulder with the second. The third shot went high and wide, because the boy started letting off shots with the Draco, spraying the microwave and the cabinets behind Flocka, and a man wearing a ski-mask popped up behind the boy, firing an AR-15 over the boy's head.

Flocka fell onto his back and scurried backward into the dining room before rushing to his feet.

In the corner of his eye, he saw wood chips kicking up from the dining table as it was shot to pieces.

He fired twice into the kitchen and then ran to the front door, tumbling over the leather sofa as he went.

His hand shook terribly as he turned the deadbolt and flung the door open. He aimed back toward the dining room and squeezed off four more shots, then ran outside and cleared the porch steps in a single bound, twisting his ankle as he landed. When he hobbled out to the sidewalk a second later, looking back at the open front door, the two policemen were out of their SUV and approaching on foot with their Glocks trained on Flocka.

"Drop the fucking weapon! Police! Freeze!"

Flocka dropped the gun but he didn't dare freeze. He limped around a parked SUV for cover, holding his hands above his head and moving as quickly as his injured ankle would allow. The policeman were on him in seconds, tackling him to the ground in the middle of the street.

"I ain't do shit, man," Flocka said as his hands were yanked behind his back.

He caught sight of the silver Chevy pickup as it came tearing out of the alley and veered left, followed closely by a black, older model Buick Regal. The cops were too focused on holding Flocka down to notice the two escaping vehicles, but Flocka kept his eye on the Buick's tail-lights until it made a turn and vanished from the night.

And then he thought: *What the fuck did I just let Whitney get me into?*

Chapter Eight

Markio's sweet day went from sugar to shit in a hurry, and it all started with three phone calls.

The first one was from his cousin Huey, and it wasn't really a serious call. Bankroll Reese, Huey's nephew, had called and told Huey about the $5 million Markio got from Worm's storage locker, and now Huey and his two brothers, Antonio "Buck" Earl and Kevin "Kay" Earl, were on their way to meet up with Markio at the Four Seasons.

Being around his older cousins was always a joy for Markio, so he didn't mind them knowing about his newfound wealth. It was the next two phone calls that put Markio in a fucked mood.

One was from his nephew Tyquan.

"You know somebody named Leezo?" Tyquan asked.

"Yeah, why?"

"He just got down on me, unc. Took my gun and that money I got from Loochie. He had like five or six other niggas with him, and all of 'em had guns. Big guns. Military-type shit. He lifted his mask and showed me his face. Said to tell you to stop hiding and come outside or he gon' kill me."

"I'm on my way," was Markio's immediate reply. "Get in the house and stay there until I pull up. And don't call your mama. Let them enjoy their vacation."

Right after Markio ended that call, pacing a tight circle in the penthouse suite's plush sitting room while Whitney stood watching him with her hands on her hips, he received a call from one person he'd never expected to call his phone..

"Hello? Markio Earl?" It was an older white man's voice, hard and authoritative.

"Yeah, this him. Who is this?"

"Martin Swiztek, Michigan City Chief of Police. I need you to tell me what the heck is going on here, and I need to do it right now. There's been another murder, right on your fucking back porch, and apparently a shootout inside your house. Now we've got a teenage kid lying dead and another mother we've got to deliver the absolute worst news to. I know this has something to do with whatever you got from that storage auction. Whitney Clarrett told us it was only clothes and furniture, but I'm having a really hard time believing that. So back to this shootout. Were you there when it went down? What did you do, run?"

"Hell no. I ain't been home since yesterday. You sure it was my house?"

Swiztek rattled off Markio's Vail Street address. "That's you, ain't it?"

Markio said nothing. He didn't know what to say and besides, he didn't cooperate with police investigations. It was the first rule of the game: no snitching, no matter what.

A glance at Whitney made him stop pacing. He squinted curiously at her, seeing something in her he'd never seen before. She looked nervous. Guilty. Like she knew something about the shootout Swiztek was asking about and didn't want to admit it.

"You need to come in and have a chat with us, if you want your name cleared from all this," Swizz said. "Give us your side of this so we can get to the root of this thing, because if you don't, we'll have no choice but to view you as a suspect."

"I ain't got no side, Swizz. I don't know shit."

"Well, at least tell me this. There's two beefs going on, right? The thing with the storage locker, and then the thing with G-Money and his boys jumping your girlfriend's son."

"I'll have my lawyer call you," Markio said, and hung up.

Whitney stared at him. He stared back at her, wondering what was going on inside that pretty head of hers. Whatever it was, he didn't trust it. He didn't trust it one bit.

"Somebody must've broke in your house," she muttered, bringing her thumb up to her mouth to nibble at the nail. A few beads of sweat had sprouted up across her forehead.

"Yeah." Markio nodded, his expression indecipherable. "They must have. Wonder what made 'em do it. Who would wanna break in my house?"

"Don't say it like that. Like I had somethin' to do with it. It probably was that bitch or one of them niggas you had all in your house yesterday."

Markio shrugged, "I didn't accuse you of nothin'. Why you so defensive?"

"Whatever." She sat down on the white fur cushion of a glass-backed chair and crossed her legs, taking her phone out her purse and looking down at it.

Markio squinted at her for a while longer, thinking over everything Swizz had just told him.

No one else had a key to his house, so how had there been a shootout inside his house and a murder on his back porch? Someone had to have broken in, and then encountered someone else there during the burglary. If someone had burglarized his house, he knew they had to be searching for the suitcases, and there were only a few people who knew the suitcases full of cash had been there. Reggie and Mya knew, but they also knew that the suitcases were no longer there. Mya had seen Markio and his guys loading the suitcases into his Benz truck before they left his house yesterday, and he'd told Reggie that he had moved them to a safer location, though he hadn't given Reggie that location.

Whitney was the only person who thought the suitcases were still at his house.

As if on cue, she looked up from her phone and said, "Ain't you worried about the suitcases? Whatever happened at your house could make the cops look around in there. And what if whoever broke in stole the suitcases? Have you thought about that?"

Markio ignored her and read a new text message: From Huey. His cousins were a few blocks away.

"Come on," he said, and turned to leave.

"I thought you said I could get a massage? And where's the rest of that money you promised me?"

"I gotta see what I lost first. I might be broke."

Whitney got up from the chair with a troubled look on her face, and she didn't say another word as they rode the elevator down to the lobby and walked out the front doors. She left him there on the sidewalk, and for the first time ever he watched her walk away without even glancing at her huge bubble butt. All the attraction was gone. She was clearly guilty of something, and Markio wanted nothing more to do with her.

He got in his brand-new Mercedes and sat there in silence, waiting for his cousins to pull up. Two minutes later they did, in the jet-black Escalade that Bankroll Reese had gifted Kay for his thirty-ninth birthday. Huey got out and joined Markio in the Benz, while Buck and Kay stood just outside Markio's open window. When he explained the situation with Leezo and what had happened to Tyquan, his cousins responded exactly the way he knew they would.

"We out there, then!" Buck exclaimed. "On Hove grave, we gon' step on his neck. Hashtag *he can't breathe no mo*. Fuck that nigga. I got in this 357 Glock with a dick and switch on that bitch. Let that nigga play crazy."

"Straight up," said Huey. "That nigga wanna rob nephew? We gon' rob his bitch ass. He mad about his lil' homies gettin' whacked? We gon' lay him down right next to them niggas."

"Say less," said Kay. He smacked the root of the Benz, and he and Buck went back to the Escalade.

As Markio drove off with Kay and Buck trailing close behind him, Huey pulled a small Ziploc type bag of loud-scented weed and a box of *White Owl* cigars from his jeans packet. He split open the cigar and dumped the tobacco in the ashtray, while Markio turned on some Polo G and cranked the volume all the way up.

Markio smoked two blunts with Huey during the forty-minute drive to Michigan City, hardly commenting on Huey's continuous praise of the new Mercedes. His mind was unwaveringly set on murdering Leezo, and he wouldn't be able to think about much else until that was done.

***

Leezo used a fork to stir the cocaine and baking soda he'd dumped into the Mason jar, wearing an N95 mask to protect himself from the fumes as he stood over the stove, cooking up two ounces of crack.

He and Markeda—the younger sister of his girlfriend, Shasta—were in the kitchen of Shasta's four-bedroom apartment in Lakeland Projects, smoking their last blunt of loud and waiting on his weed man to arrive with more smoke.

Behind the mask, the corners of Leezo's mouth were turned up in a victorious smile. He had wanted to kill Markio himself, but Ikey had done it for him, using the Draco to splatter Markio's brains all over the back porch. When Ikey started shooting at Markio's friend inside the house, Leezo had stood over Markio's body and shot him three more times in the head with the AR-15 that had belonged to Polo.

He'd joined in the gunfight when he realized Ikey was hit, firing the AR-15 over Ikey's head, but because he'd been forced to bob and weave as the boy inside the house returned fire, his aim hadn't been all that accurate.

Now Ikey was at the local hospital. They'd dropped him off in front of the Emergency Room doors and sped off in the stolen Buick, only to stop in an alleyway three blocks down to get out and set the Buick ablaze. Afterward, Leezo drove to Shasta's apartment and brought his guns inside before allowing the gang to head back to Chicago in his pickup, which had never truly been his from the start. He'd carjacked the Silverado in Chicago the previous summer and paid one of his homies to swap out the VIN numbers with a wrecked Silverado of the same color to make it seem legitimate. He'd used the pickup in multiple shootings today, and now he wanted nothing more to do with it.

Leezo removed the Mason jar from the pot of boiling water and set it aside to let it cool off and harden. Then he went to the kitchen table, where his box of sandwich bags and a digital scale lay next to a plastic ashtray, and sat down with Markeda.

"What time your sister get off work?" he asked. His chair was on the same side of the table as Markeda's, facing her, and he made no attempt at concealing his gaze as he stared at her thighs. They looked particularly thick in the snug-fitting yellow sundress she had on.

"Four-thirty," Markeda answered. She lowered his mask and put the blunt to his lips, and he sucked in a mouthful of smoke. "We're supposed to be going to the beach when she get off. Our sister Kela and all her kids gon' be there."

Leezo was wearing latex gloves to keep the cocaine residue off his hand and out of his pores.

As he inhaled the weed smoke and held it in, he placed his gloved hands on Markeda's knees and spread her legs apart, so he could get a good look at her fat, naked pussy.

"You know I got a man, Leezo. We can't keep doing this."

"Fuck that nigga. I heard he a rat, anyway." Leezo reached between her parted thighs, but she grabbed his wrist to stop him.

"Nooo. I can't, Leez. I can't keep being nasty like that. My sister would kill me if she knew I was fucking her man, and my boyfriend would probably kill me, too." She pushed Leezo's hand from between her thighs and snapped them shut. "Mickey eats my pussy every time he walks through that door. Last time me and you fucked, you didn't pull out when you nutted, and I had to sit on my man's face after that. Do you have any idea how nasty I felt doing that? No. Uh-uh. I can't do that again."

Lezzo chuckled dryly and blew a stream of smoke at Markeda's pretty round face. She was pecan-brown and much thicker than her older sister Shasta. She waved the smoke away and flipped him a middle finger, so he spread her legs again and shoved two fingers deep inside her pussy.

"Stop, Leezo. I'm serious," she said, but she let out a low moan that Leezo took as permission to keep at it, so he kept sliding his fingers in and out of her gushy center, even as she struggled to push his hand away.

When he finally took his fingers out of her, the blue latex that covered them was slippery with her creamy vaginal juices. He removed the gloves and stood up, the front of his black sweatpants sticking out before him. He dug in his pocket and brought out the cash he'd taken from Markio's nephew. He'd counted it out. It was exactly five thousand dollars.

"Look at all this," he said, fanning through the cash. There were numerous hundreds, fifties, and twenties, and even more tens, fives, and ones, making the pile of cash look more like twenty grand instead of the five grand it was. "I'll give you two hundred right now for some of that pussy."

"Leezo," Markeda said, as if she were fed up with him. But her eyes remained on the cash, and she opened her legs a few inches wider. "Shit, that is a lot of money. How much money is that?"

Leezo gave her no answer. He spread the cash out on the table and pulled Markeda to her feet, turning her toward the table and bending her over it.

"Count it for me," he said, hiking up her sundress with one hand and freeing his erection

He slid into her tight pussy and began fucking her roughly, holding her wrist in both hands as he slammed in and out of her. His dick was only six inches in length, but he had enough girth to make all his hoes scream out his name, which is what Markeda was doing when the doorbell rang three minutes later.

Leezo slid all the way in and held it there as he took out his phone. His weed man had just texted him: *'I'm at the door.'*

'One minute', Leezo texted hack, rubbing Markeda's voluminous ass as he did it.

He pocketed his smartphone and continued fucking Markeda. As it turned out, he was right on time. Exactly one minute later, he clenched his narrow butt cheeks tightly together as his dick twitched and spurted out a copious load, and once again he failed to pull out.

***

Mickey Shipman had been a confidential informant for the Michigan City Police Department since January of 2014, and in the ensuing eight years he'd assisted the drug task force in thirty-two arrests, all of which had led to felony convictions for the dope boys he set up.

But this was the first time they'd asked him to set up a murder suspect.

He was thinking of a way to entrap Markio Earl when he drove past a sleek black Mercedes sedan as he entered Lakeland Projects. He parked his sky-blue 1994 Chevy Caprice behind a candy-painted dark blue 1987 Caprice on gold Forgiato rims. The flashy Caprice's owner was Reginald "Reggie" Flight, a coal-black weed dealer who'd heard all about Mickey being a C. I. Mickey had tried to get him twice already, but Reggie always swore he'd given up hustling after his last bid in federal prison.

Reggie was standing outside the door to the apartment where Mickey's girlfriend Markeda lived with her older sister Shasta, and just as Mickey was walking up behind Reggie, the front door opened and Shasta's boyfriend, Leezo, pushed open the screen door to let Reggie in.

"Markeda here? "Mickey asked, rubbing the screen door before it could slam shut in his face.

Leezo only looked at him. Reggie turned and regarded Mickey with the same cold stare, but neither man spoke to him. Instead, Leezo shouted for Markeda, and he and Reggie walked off toward the kitchen.

When Markeda made it to the door, she was pushing two hundred-dollar bills down into her Michael Kors bag. Mickey frowned at the money, wondering how she'd gotten it.

"Where you get that from?" he asked. "You just asked me to bring you some money so you can go to the beach with Shasta."

"My uncle Tony brought it to me. Come on, let's go upstairs," she said, taking his hand and leading him into the apartment.

Mickey's eyes were everywhere as he walked through the living room to climb the stairs; he glanced into the kitchen. Leezo and Reggie were out of sight, but there was a box of sandwich bags and a digital scale on the small square table, and Mickey knew exactly what that meant. There were drugs somewhere in there.

"What Reggie doin' over here?" Mickey asked, rubbing his hands all over Markeda's fat ass cheeks as she climbed the stairs ahead of him. "Leezo coppin' from him or some'n?"

"I have no idea, Mickey. That is none of my business."

Mickey tried lifting the hem of her sundress before they reached the top of the staircase.

She smacked his hand away and rushed into the bathroom.

"Let me pee first," she said, and closed the door in his face.

Mickey's hand shot to the doorknob and turned it before she could lock him out. He shoved the door, and Markeda laughed as he barged into the bathroom with her. "Now you can lock the door," he said, closing his arms around her waist and kissing her on the neck.

"I need to wash up, Mickey. I don't want you going down there when I've been walking in the sun all morning."

"I like that smell." He pulled up her sundress and palmed her fluffy butt cheeks, then leaned back against the sink and reached over to push the door shut. He pulled out his phone. "We need to talk anyway. I might have to set somebody else up."

"You need to stop doing that shit, Mickey. You could get killed out here."

"Baby, these niggas kill nothin'. And I ain't start settin' niggas up until one of 'em set me up. Plus, the police been payin' me five hundred dollars every time I wire up and make me a buy. We need that money, baby. You know it like I know it. That money paid for your wardrobe. That money paid your bond when you got locked up for shoplifting. And remember when your cousin died from smokin' that weed he bought that was laced with Fentanyl? I'm the one who set up the nigga who sold him that shit. "

"Get a fucking job, Mickey," Markeda muttered, crossing her arms and pouting.

On his Samsung smartphone, Mickey accessed his Facebook page, searched for Markio Earl, and typed out a message. '*My uncle in the G got $2200 for a zip of some good H*'. He sent the message and looked up at Markeda. There were tears in her eyes. Her lower lip was quivering. She went to the toilet, lifted her sundress, and sat down, presumably to pee.

"It's embarrassing, Mickey," she said. "It's fucking embarrassing knowing my boyfriend is working with the police. It stresses me out."

"They just offered me five grand to set up one person, baby." Mickey walked over to her and lifted her chin so he could look in her eyes. "I swear to God. Five thousand dollars."

"It's not worth the risk, Mickey. It's just not. And you got me lookin' stupid out here. A lot of my friends won't talk to me no more."

"Fuck what these bitches got to say about you! It's about us! We can use that five thousand from this raggedy ass city. You said you wanted to move down to Dallas, right? That five racks will hold us over until we find somewhere to work."

Markeda sniffled as a small amount of urine trickled out of her. She dumped the tears from her eyes and sighed. "Who, Mickey? Who do they want you to set up this time?"

"Markio."

Markeda's eyebrows crawled up onto her forehand like two fast-moving black caterpillars.

Her back straightened, and she moved back on the toilet, as if Mickey had contracted a new variant of COVID-19 that was a thousand times deadlier than the original virus. She pulled some tissue from the roll and wiped herself.

"No, Mickey. No, no, no." She got up from the toilet and flushed. "Not him. He's not the kind of person you can set up and forget about. He'll do something."

"I know who he is. I remember when he used to shoot shit up all the time. He ain't the only nigga with a gun." Mickey put his hands on Markeda's hips and picked her up, carrying her to the sink and sitting her down on the ledge. "You don't need to worry about me, baby. I'm good. "God ain't made a nigga who can fuck with me."

Markeda still looked worried, but Mickey could care less. He was a Gangster Disciple from one of the roughest hoods in Gary, Indiana. He'd shot and wounded several men in his younger days. He'd robbed drug dealers at gunpoint and sold ounces upon ounces of cocaine. As far as Mickey was concerned, he was just as street as Markio, and if it came down to gunplay, he was more than willing to shoot it out. Especially since he had the police on his team.

He went to his knees between Markeda's thick thighs and ran his tongue between her pussy lips. She tasted extra creamy today, as wet as she'd been a few days ago when he had her sit on his face. More of her tangy cream oozed out onto his tongue as he sucked and licked on her fat pussy lips. He swallowed hungrily and then went up to suck on her clitoris while he fingered her.

Markeda had just begun to moan and gyrate her hips in tune with Mickey's flickering tongue when a rapid thunder of fully-automatic gunfire shattered the moment.

Chapter Nine

"You know I just got that nigga Markio knocked off," Leezo had said casually. "About an hour ago. Lil' Folks knocked his head off with a Draco.

"Yeah?" Reggie forced a smile that showed all his gold squares of teeth. He'd been standing beside Leezo at the kitchen counter, watching as Leezo counted out $3,000 to buy a half pound of Black Cherry Gelato from him. "What you do that for?"

"He the one who whacked G-Money yesterday. D-Nut saw him do it. Think that's why he got D-Nut and Polo whacked last night."

Reggie shrugged his broad shoulders, feigning indifference. "Fuck that nigga. I don't even know him like that."

"On Larry," Leezo said, pausing to throw up the "rakes," a gang sign for the Gangster Disciples that resembled a pitchfork and was made by sticking up the middle finger between the thumb and forefinger. "It's GD till the world blow. Fuck that hook-ass nigga."

He'd still been counting a few seconds later—"A'ight, that's twenty-three hundred right there…"—when the distant sound of the screen door opening in the living room made him look up.

"Go see who that is, Folks," Leezo said.

Reggie had nodded, already knowing who it was, and then only stepped aside as Markio and his three cousins stormed into the kitchen, their guns trained on Leezo.

"Who said I was hiding?" Markio asked, aiming the Micro Draco at Leezo's face. "They lied to you, fam. I ain't never hid from no nigga."

Reggie started scooping up the money from the counter and dropping it into his white leather backpack, and Leezo looked from him to Markio, his eyes as wide as saucers.

"You bitch-ass nigga," he said to Reggie, once it all came together in his head.

"Nah, you just a dumb-ass nigga. You had Melvo killed, not Markio. How you gon' try to get a nigga whacked when you don't even know what he look like?" Reggie turned to Markio. "Be careful, bruh. That police-ass nigga Mickey Shipman upstairs."

85

Markio nodded and rolled down his ski-mask. His cousins already had theirs pulled down over their faces, and all four of them wore black leather gloves.

Markio waited for Reggie to leave the apartment before he nudged Kay with an elbow and said, "Go up there and kill that rat." Leezo raised his hand. "Wait. Wait a minute. Look, I'll leave right now. I'll go back to—"

"Fuck all that waitin'," said Buck, as he aimed his Talock 32 at Leezo's face and squeezed the trigger.

The rapid gunfire sounded like it came from a gargantuan rattlesnake. Nearly every round hit Leezo in the face, and Markio opened fire with the Draco, sending a dozen 7.62-millimeter projectiles through Leezo's head, neck, and upper chest. Two of Leezo's long dreads were blown from his scalp and became glued to the wall four feet behind him. His head was blown to pieces.

Huey turned away from the gruesome attack, disgusted by the sight of it.

As soon as they stopped shooting, there was more rapid gunfire upstairs, followed by a woman's horrified screams. Kay came running back down the stairs, and the four of them ran outside to the burgundy Grand Am they'd stolen at gunpoint from an elderly man a few blocks away. Markio got behind the wheel and sped off, trying not to look at all the people who were running scared, their previously peaceful summer afternoon interrupted by the frightening sounds of warfare.

Mya was waiting at the front of the apartment complex in Markio's S-Class Mercedes, and it didn't look suspicious when she raced off ahead of the Gorand Am full of masked gunmen because several other vehicles were also fleeing the apartment complex. They stopped near the middle school around the corner, where Kay had parked his Escalade, and left the Pontiac Sedan idling there as they shot off in different directions, Mya and Markio in the Mercedes, Markio's three cousins in the Escalade.

Markio reclined in the passenger seat and snatched off his mask and gloves. He dropped them and his Micro Draco into the shopping bags on the backseat.

"You can't just keep using me for this crazy shit," Mya said, but she looked excited, her juicy lips upturned in her signature smile. She was dressed professionally in a gray designer skirt and a silky black blouse over gray Louboutin heels. Her hair was colored blond and out in a neat little bob. Her fingernails were pointed like claws and painted gray, like the skirt. "I just sold two houses this morning—one for $235,000 and another for $309,000—and now you got me playing getaway driver, fleeing the scene of God knows what."

"You ain't fleein' the scene of nothin'. You're just driving, so just drive." Markio fired up a Newports ciggie and lowered his window a crack as Mya drove, and he didn't turn on his phone until they were back on the highway five minutes later.

He texted Huey and told him they'd meet back up at the Four Seasons. Then he texted Nikkia and told her about the burglary at his house and the murder that had taken place on his back porch. Every time he looked up from his phone, he saw Mya staring at him, and there was a glossy, dreamy look to her light brown eyes.

"If you don't pay attention to the goddamn road," he said, and pulled on his cigarette.

"I'm sorry." She giggled softly." It's just that I love that gangsta shit. I mean, I told you that already. The shit is a turn-on. You got me wet as fuck right now."

Markio was about to say something back when his phone rang. It was Nikkia calling. He put in his AirPods; Mya wouldn't hear Nikkia's half of the conversation.

"What's up, sweet lady?" he answered, blowing cigarette smoke out his tinted window.

"Another murder?" Nikkia's sexy voice dipped with disbelief. "You've got to be kidding me."

"I was in Chicago when it happened."

"Yeah, well, you can't tell the police that. You're not supposed to leave the state. But you know what? This might actually help you."

"How can a murder that happened at my house help me?"

"I just filed a motion with the court out there asking for what's called an *Emergency Interstate Compact*. It's a request to have your parole switched over to another state within the next twenty-four hours. I implied that your life may be in danger, and I cited the ongoing conflict in Michigan City. Now that your house has been burglarized and a murder has taken place on your back porch when you weren't even home, the EIC is almost certain to be granted."

"Don't I have to have a new address to give the court?"

"Yes, you do. I put down the address to a condo I own in Streeterville. You can stay there for now. It's furnished and everything."

"And where is Streeterville? I ain't never heard of no goddamn Streeterville."

"It's in Chicago. Just—probably not where you're used to hanging out. Not many black people there, though. Oprah used to own a condo in the same building where my condo is located. We'll talk about all that later. I have a Zoom meeting with your judge and the prosecuting attorney in ten minutes."

"Okay. Just call me back. See, I knew I hired you for a reason."

"Yeah, yeah, whatever. You'd just better be ready for me when I get to the hotel suite. We're turning off our phones as soon as I walk through the door. I don't want any interruptions. We clear on that?"

Markio looked over at Mya. She was staring at him again. He pointed forcefully at the windshield, and she snickered guiltily as she turned her eyes back to the road.

"I got you, sweet lady," he said to Nikkia. "Just take care of that court hearing for me."

"Okay, gotta go. See you soon."

"Who was that?" Mya asked as soon as the call ended.

"My lawyer." Markio saw that he had several new messages on Facebook Messenger and clicked on the app, only to find that two of the seven new messages were from men he knew were confidential informants. "What the fuck?" he murmured aloud to himself.

"What is it?" Mya asked.

"Hold up."

"You sure do talk nice to that lawyer of yours. I never heard anybody call their lawyer, '*sweet lady*'. What kind of lawyer is she?"

Markio blew off the comment, clicked on the message from Mickey Shipman and shook his head incredulously when he finished reading it. What were the odds that Mickey had messaged him just minutes before he'd sent Kay upstairs in Shasta's apartment to kill the rat?

The second inbox message was from Damian Middlebrooks, another known rat: "*Bro this Dame from Normandy Village. My nigga told me to holla at you. I got 2 stamps for sale, a glock 40 and kel-tec 9. You can get 'em both for $450. I heard you got beef wit g money ppl. What yall get n2 it about anyway? Get back at me bro 1.*"

The other five messages were from family members who'd heard about the five million dollars Markio had gotten out of Worm's storage locker—Mariah and Shakia, his two younger sisters; Bankroll Reese's sister—Chanel—and Huey's daughter Tinky; and Markio's older brother, Lil' Bill. But Markio was far too preoccupied with the messages from the informants to reply to his family. He'd never gotten a message from Dame or Mickey until today and he found it odd that two known snitches would message him back to back, within the same hour.

He was reading the message from Mickey Shipman for the third time when another message came through, this one from Keyshawn Bradley, a twenty-year-old hustler who'd copped heroin from Markio a couple of times last year. The last he'd heard, Keyshawn had been busted for dealing heroin to an undercover cop sometime in May.

'*Lords you still got grams for $80? If so I'll grab thirty of em,*'

Markio started laughing when he figured out what was going on. "They're tryin' way too hard," he said, blowing his cigarette out the window. "Too-too hard."

"Who's trying too hard?" Mya asked.

"Twelve. They got all these rats messaging me, tryna get me to buy guns and sell 'em dope and shit. Anything to get me to slip up. I an't goin', though, toot me fucked up."

He lay back in his set and closed his eyes. He was still high off the weed he'd smoked with Huey. The high helped him think better, helped him strategize and figure things out.

"I gave Nissa that eight thousand dollars I got from your boy Crasher last night," Mya said, "so all you owe her now is two thousand. I'll send it to her myself if you want me to."

Markio only nodded. He was thinking about Dame and Keyshawn. If the police were going to use them to get at him, then he would strike first. He would make the police wish they'd come up with a better plan than using two low-level rats to try to trip him up.

His eyes popped open at the sound of his phone ringing, and he answered a *FaceTime* call from his boy Sway Swanson.

"I could be a fake-ass nigga and tell you we did it, but I ain't built like that," Sway said and Markio instantly knew what he was talking about. "Somebody just slumped Leezo in Lakeland. Him and Mickey Shipman. Markeda all on Instagram cryin' how somebody whacked Mickey right in front of her."

"Damn, for real?" Markio said, acting surprised.

"You want that ten racks back?" Sway asked.

"Nah. I got two other niggas I need y'all to talk to," Markio said, taking the last pull on his cigarette and sitting forward to stub it out in the ashtray. "You know Lil' Keyshawn from East Chicago and Dame from Normandy Village?"

***

Huey or one of his brothers must have alerted the rest of The Earls to their imminent arrival, because half of the Earl Family was already there when they walked into the Four Seasons Hotel lobby. Markio's two younger sisters, Mariah and Shakia, were the first to rush in for hugs. Then came his beautiful albino cousin: Chanel, and her lovely mother—Rose, who'd just turned fifty but still looked thirty. Rose's other two children, Bankroll Reese and former Miami Heat player Rodney "Hot Rod" James, were just as happy to see Maria as he was to see them. Huey's two adult children, Khalil and Khalace, better known as Tits and Tinky, were also present, as well as Kay's daughter—Kayshawn. They had already gone and purchased half a dozen fifths of D'usse and several cases of beer, and the drinks started flowing mere seconds after they walked into the spacious inviting penthouse suite.

Kay, Buck, and Huey had carried in Markio's shopping bags, while Markio held on to his cash-filled duffels. He took the duffel bags into the massive all-white bedroom and took out two $50,000 bundles of hundreds for his sisters. With Bankroll Reese's forty-million-dollar net worth and the $22 million Rodney had gotten from the NBA, Rose and her children were well taken care of, but Markio still gave Chanel and Rose $25,000 bundles of fifties. He offered the same amount to the others, emptying his two duffels of fifty dollar bills. Only Reese and Rodney turned down the cash, and Markio gave their share to Kayshawn and Tinky.

After a while, Markio stepped away to the bathroom to answer a *FaceTime* call from Nikkia. He stood the phone up against the wall on the white marble sink, and Nikkia took a long moment to look him over, biting down on her bottom lip as she watched him study his reflection in the mirror. He looked at the phone screen and blew a kiss at the sexy faced attorney.

"Can you say success?" Nikkia asked, a triumphant smirk raising the corners of her pretty mouth.

"I believe I can. Why? Do I need to?"

"You absolutely do. The EIC has been granted. Judge Lang and I go way back to my rookie days in the courtroom, and as soon as I mentioned that there had been a homicide on your back porch when you weren't even home, she granted the motion. You'll have to appear with me for a video hearing tomorrow at noon, but as of now you're officially an Illinois resident. Congratulations."

"Thank you so much, sweet lady, even though I think you only filed that motion to get me back in Chicago for your own dirty lil' reasons," Markio said, beaming a 1,000 watt smile.

"I might have." She knitted her brow. "What's all that music I hear?"

"Don't kill me," he said, "but my daddy's family slid through on me. You know it's been a minute since they last saw me."

"Great, that's even better. It just means I won't have to wait to meet your family. As long as you don't have any crazy exes there, we're cool."

Markio's mouth opened to say something, but no words came out. His mouth just stayed that way, opened wide, until Nikkia gave him a tight-eyed look.

"One of your exes is there?" she asked snappishly.

"Not exactly," he explained. "She's the girl who saved my life last night. She shot up the nigga who shot me in the leg—well, shot me in the cash. She ain't my ex. I just met her at a gas station three days ago. We did fuck at my crib in MC yesterday, and she gave me some head at the Marriott last night. That's it, though. I swear."

"Hm." One corner of Nikkia's mouth drew back, a clear sign of skepticism. "What does she look like? I bet she's big and ugly and just—ugh! Why would you invite her over anyway when you knew I was coming?"

"Okay, first off, I don't fuck no big ugly bitches, as we can get that straight right now. Shorty bad as fuck, on my mama. Secondly, she shot a nigga for me last night and she just found out he didn't make it. She was all sad and shit. I couldn't just leave her alone."

Nikkia still looked skeptical, so Markio continued on his pursuit to capture her heart, because she was the one woman he'd wanted all his life.

"Listen," he said, picking up the phone, "on everything I love, I will make her leave right now, or as soon as you get here, if you feel any way about her being here. I would never disrespect you, Nikkia. I can't lie, I thought about fuckin' with Mya—that's her name—I thought about fuckin' with her the long way, but that was before I saw you again. You're the one for me. I know it. Please don't let this one fucked up decision I made mess this up."

"Awww," Nikkia cooed, her eyes glowing with love. "Well, thank you. I think you might be the one for me, too. And you don't have to make her leave. You know, I've dabbled with women a time or two. Maybe she can join us in the bedroom. As long as it's made clear that I'm the main lady. I'm sure we can find room for her."

"See what I mean?" Markio said, his smile turning up another thousand watts. "That's how I know you're the one for me. I'm buying you a ring ASAP. We don't even need to wait. We can go down to the courthouse tomorrow and get married."

Nikkia laughed hard at that, rolling her pretty eyes and shaking her head. "I can't with you. I just can't. You are too much for me and I cannot deal."

"Yes, you can, I'll help along." Markio laughed, too, adjusting his Louis Vuitton bucket hat. "How long before you get here?"

"I have one more business matter to handle and then I'm free. I'll text you when I get there and you'd better meet me outside at my car. I'm not about to be looking like some side chick walking in there. I'm sorry, but that's just one of my things."

"Say no more. I'll be waiting at the curb with a dozen roses."

"Oh, shut up. Bye," Nikkia said, and hung up on him.

Markio pumped his fist triumphantly as the call ended. He went out to the sitting room, picked up the hotel room phone, and requested a dozen long-stemmed red roses from room service. He would be a man of his word from the very start with Nikkia Staples, doing everything it took to make her happy and keep her that way, because although he was a gangsta through and through, he was no different than any other black man in the sense that he wanted a beautiful black woman to come home to every day and night, a drop-dead gorgeous black queen he could call his own, and Nikkia Staples was the queen for him.

Chapter Ten

"Seven murders in two fucking days. This is unreal," Chief Swiztek said to Lieutenant Corley as they stood outside the open front door to Shasta Crosby's apartment in Lakeland Project, looking around at the spectators who were gathered on the sidewalk across the street holding up their smartphones to record videos of the crime scene.

"Make that eight," said Corley. "The victim from last night's hotel shooting didn't pull through."

Swizz turned his back on the crowd of onlookers and chewed on the corner of his bottom lip, his head slowly and subtly moving from left to right as he struggled to wrap his head around the whole big shit-show. There was a lot of shit in the show to take in.

"The guy who was dumped at the hospital earlier," he said. "What's with him?"

"He's from Chicago just like the guy who took us on a chase yesterday after Whitney Clarrett shot him. Claims he was walking down an alley when he was shot, but I'm willing to bet he was involved in that shootout at Markio's place."

"And we still haven't spotted that fucking Mercedes truck?"

"Nope. No sign of it. If Markio's behind all this, he's a lot smarter than we're giving him credit for. Maybe he learned some stuff in prison. Learned how to do his dirt and get away with it."

"I want him brought in for questioning. I don't care if he does lawyer up. A teenager was murdered on his back porch. He has to know something."

Detective Mulberry came walking out of the apartment with an identification card pinched between her gloved thumb and forefinger. "The guy in the kitchen is Bartholomew Thompson, age twenty-eight. From Chicago, and he looks a lot like the fourth suspect in that assault on Whitney Clarrett's kid."

Swizz studied the Illinois ID. There was no doubt about it Bartholomew Thompson was the fourth assault suspect. Now every single one of the four men who'd assaulted seventeen-year old James Thomas, Jr. were dead.

"The vic upstairs is Mickey Shipman. One of our best informants," said Mulberry. "I had just talked with him about going after Markio Earl. He said he believed he could get it done, and I offered him five grand. He was dead ten minutes later."

Mulberry's smart phone rang, and she stepped aside to answer it, her blond hair blowing in the breeze.

"The Grand Am they used to get away was reportedly taken in an armed carjacking a few minutes before the shooting," Corley said, "The carjackers wore gloves and ski-masks, same as they did when they ran in here."

Swizz was nodding thoughtfully and processing the info when Mulberry rejoined them.

"Shasha Crosby and her sister, Markeda, arrived at the station about twenty minutes ago. Markeda was apparently in the upstairs bathroom with Mickey when all this went down. She's saying the guy who killed him opened the bathroom door, called Mickey a rat-ass-n-word, and then shot him dead. We've got a bunch of shell casings in the kitchen, sixteen from a 357 and twelve from a 7.62 rifle, and ten more .357 shell casings in the hallway outside the upstairs bathroom. Nearly all of them were headshots. These guys didn't stand a chance."

"Jesus Christ," Swizz muttered. "What the hell is going on here?"

And just when he thought things couldn't possibly get any worse, his phone rang with a call from Keith Flynn, prosecuting attorney for superior court 1, the courtroom for top-tier felons like Markio Earl.

"Got some bad news for ya," Flynn said. "You're gonna hate to hear it, but here it goes. Markio Earl is no longer an Indiana citizen. He's just had his parole switched over to Illinois. So unless you can come up with some real hard evidence to charge him with one of these murders there's nothing more we can do with him."

"Are you fucking kidding me right now?"

"Wish I was. I fought it with everything I had, but he's hired Nikkia Staples. Nobody beats her in the courtroom. She's got a golden tongue. As of today, Markio Earl's official residence is a three-million-dollar condominium in one of the wealthiest zip codes in Chicago."

"Son of a bitch!" Swizz exclaimed, ending the call in a rage. He took off his glasses and pinched the bridge of his nose. Squeezed his eyes shut. Tried to calm his nerves.

"Is everything okay?" Mulberry asked.

Swizz opened his eyes and looked at her. Tiny black spots danced in his vision. The temperature seemed to have grown ten degrees hotter. He could almost feel his blood pressure rising higher and higher by the second as he held his smart phone in a death grip.

"I want you to contact every informant we have," he said, speaking slowly and concisely. "I'm authorizing a ten-thousand dollar payment to anyone who can get the fucker Markio Earl on tape confessing to his involvement in one of these murders."

***

The man Detective Mulberry had texted asking him to meet her down at the station was already seated in Interview Room 3 when she arrived. Waddell Flemingston still had on his painter's overalls, with dollops of white and gray paint splattered all over his walnut-brown skin. He was snacking on a bag of pork skins, with a cold can of sprite dripping condensation onto the square wood table in front of him. He had the whole room smelling like paint, pork, and musty underarms.

"Good afternoon, Mr. Flemingston," Mulberry said, deliberately activating her sexually suggestive smile as she shut the door and sat down across from him.

"Aww shit. What I do this time?" he asked, his jaws working overtime on the pork skins.

"Nooo. You didn't do anything. I just have a couple of questions I thought you might be able to help me out with."

"Questions? What kind of questions?" Waddell looked worried.

"Well, we've had eight homicides in two days—including a double homicide that just went down in Lakeland Projects, your old stomping grounds, and we don't have anyone in custody. If we don't get someone in custody soon, we're gonna have to start cracking down on the whole city."

"I go to work and come home, Mulberry. I swear I've been workin' twelve-hour shifts all week. I don't know shit."

Waddell put down the bag of pork skins to scratch his forearm. Mulberry knew he was fighting an opioid addiction that was currently being treated with Subaxane, which made him itch continuously. She knew he had a fiancée, a two-year-old daughter and a seven-month-old son, and that he and Markio Earl used to be close friends.

And above all else she knew his secret: that last year he had allowed the DEA to wire him up with a hidden camera and an audio recorder in a drug deal for five kilos of cocaine that had helped send a high-ranking Black P. Stone to Federal prison with a 480-month sentence.

"How much did the DEA pay you to take down Red Mae?" Mulberry asked.

As expected, Waddell's head jerked back in surprise, and he looked at Mulberry with a certain level of trepidation in his cool brown eyes.

"Yeah," she said, "I know all about that. Just tell me. Did they pay you? Did they offer you ten grand to wire up for them? Because that's how much is on the table here."

Waddell hesitated; then: "They didn't pay me nothin'. I got caught up in a wiretap. They had me on the phone asking Red Mae's girl for a nine piece, and they pulled me over right after I picked it up. I had a stolen gun in the car with me, a fully automatic. I would've went Fed if I hadn't set him up. They offered to get rid of the gun and the dope case and they was already on to him anyway so I went ahead and did it." He scratched an elbow. "How in the hell did you find that out?"

"I have my sources." Mulberry took out her smartphone, pulled up a mugshot of Markio Earl, and showed it to Waddell. "What can you tell me about this guy?"

"Aw, that's Kio. That used to be my lil' nigga in Lakeland. He really ran with my lil brother—Dot, but I fucked with him, too. He fuckin' with Whitney sexy ass now." Waddell picked up his can of Sprite and took two loud gulps. Then, putting the can down, he said, "What was that you said about ten grand? Y'all throwin' that kinda money around?"

"We have reason to believe that Markio Earl shot and killed Gregory Samuels on West 7th Street yesterday afternoon. We also believe he had a hand in last night's double homicide on 6th and Cedar, and maybe even the second double homicide that just took place in Lakeland."

"Waddell's brow rose, and he took another swallow of Sprite. "Goddamn," he paused, taking it in. "But you know what? I ain't even surprised. That lil' nigga been crazy like that, you know, he killed a nigga in Lakeland when he was like eleven years old. Stomped that boy to death. I watched him do it. They sent him to juvenile and he was right back on the streets like a year later."

"Would you consider wiring on him?"

"For ten thousand dollars?"

Mulberry nodded. "We're offering ten thousand dollars to anyone who can get Markio Earl to confess to his involvement in at least one of these murders. As long as you get it recorded, you'll get paid. I will personally wire the money to your bank account. So what do you think? You up to it?"

"Shiit," Wadell said, really dragging out the word. "For ten thousand dollars, I'll set up my own mama. Just tell me what I need to do. Let me go home and wash all this paint off me, and I'll be ready to roll."

***

Although their mother, Ms. Pat, had passed away six years ago, the Swanson siblings—Sway, Shannon, and Stephanie—were closer than ever. Steph worked as a cook at Indiana State Prison and as a side hustle she snuck in taped-up packages of drugs and cell phones for a few of the inmates which made her upwards of

$10,000-a-month, money that she split evenly with Shannon and Sway.

Steph was the only one of the Swanson siblings with an actual job. Shannon and Sway were drug dealers. Their main hustle was weed, but every now and then they sold other drugs. Now, though with the $40,000 Markio had paid them for whacking Polo and D-Nut last night (and the extra $10,000 Markio had left in the rubber-banded pile of hundreds as half the payment for them to whack Leezo), they were seriously considering giving up hustling to become full-time hit men.

They were in a 1973 Buick Roadmaster they rented from a crack-head called Lawnmower Man, drinking from a cold bottle of Aquafina water and rolling off ecstasy pills as they sat parked outside of Chris Diggs' barber shop on Michigan Boulevard. Inside the barber shop, seated in a chair near the window, was Keyshawn Bradley.

"We should just shoot him through the window," Sway said, tying his dreadlocks back in a knot.

"Nigga, what you think this is, Superfly? We ain't tryna whack the Sno' Patrol. And we can't shoot up the barber shop. I get my hair cut in there every other week.

"You should lock your shit up like mine."

"I don't want no dreadlocks." Shannon closed his right hand around the Glock on his lap. His skin tone was a lot darker than Sway's but they were both 6'3" and essentially the same build. Looking at the Glock, Shannon added, "Let's just wait for him to leave out. I'll hang out the window and get him then. Hit him all in his head, then we'll be another ten racks up."

Two seconds later, an MCPD patrol car drove past with the emergency lights on, pulling over a dark red Cadillac with tinted windows. It was the fourth time they'd seen someone get pulled over in the last hour. The MCPD was on a traffic stopping spree.

"It might be too hot out here to start shootin'," Shannon said worriedly.

Sway nodded his agreement and the two of them looked over at Keyshawn as he came walking out of the barber shop with a fresh cut, wearing a red Nike T-shirt and shorts that looked much too tight on his short, thick legs. He went walking north up the sidewalk, pausing to raise his smart phone and snap a selfie before continuing on, not a care in the world.

"Don't he live somewhere around here?" Shannon asked.

"Fuck if I know." Sway started the car and pulled slowly away from the curb as Keyshawn made it to the corner and turned east onto the side street. "I wonder where Markio got all that money from. That nigga can't be raced up like that from sellin' bows. I think he paid Nissa for that drop last night too, "cause she just went and bought a brand-new Charger."

Shannon had nothing to say to that. He didn't care where Markio got the money from. All that mattered was how much of it Markio gave to them, and apparently Markio wasn't done giving. He'd put the extra $10,000 he gave them last night on Keyshawn's head and another 10,000 on Dame's head.

Sway turned onto the side street just as Keyshawn was stepping off the curb to cross to the other side of the street. Keyshawn had his head down, looking at his phone, and he held up a hand to the approaching Roadmaster like a crossing guard, urging them to wait for him to cross the street.

"Fuck it, run him over," Shannon said.

And Sway did just that, stamping down on the gas and speeding right toward the arrogant young millennial. Keyshawn tried to step back and fell, and the passenger's side tires rolled right over his belly, flipping him over in the process.

Sway hit the brakes and looked in the rearview mirror, while Shannon looked back over his headrest. Keyshawn lay broken in the idle of the street, twisted and motionless, but Sway wasn't taking any chances. He reversed over the chubby young hustler and then drove forward bumping over him a third time before speeding away.

Chapter Eleven

Nikkia didn't pull up until 5:35 p.m. And as promised, Markio was outside waiting for her with a dozen long-stemmed red roses, dressed in white Jordan 5 sneakers, white Amiri jeans, and a white Givenchy T-shirt. He'd stopped at a nearby jewelry store and purchased himself two $15,000 diamond necklaces, and Nikkia stared at them as the valet took the key tab to her Bentley convertible. Then her gaze shifted to the roses, and she accepted them with a growing smile, lowering her nose to one rose to inhale its lovely fragrance.

"Look at you. All nice and romantic," she said.

Markio took her hand, interlacing his fingers with hers so they could walk into the hotel together. "Anything to make you happy," he said, really meaning it. "My family's still here, but I got a second room for us. It's a honeymoon suite. Got a heart-shaped bed with rose petals on it, mirrors all around the bedroom, a champagne bucket with a bottle of Ace of Spades on ice. The whole nine."

"Okay," Nikkia said, sounding genuinely impressed. "You pulled out all the stops. I see your effort. It's duly noted."

Markio leaned in and kissed her on the cheek. She smelled as good, and she looked even better, a caramel-brown goddess with hips like a coke bottle. He couldn't believe it—he actually had Nikkia Staples by his side, the girl of his dreams walking hand in hand with him. In prison, he had fantasized about the moment a thousand times—not necessarily this exact moment, but numerous variations of it—but those imaginations paled in comparison to the reality of having such a gorgeous, sophisticated woman in his presence. Her snow-white dress fit her like a second skin. The strap of her white leather Hermes Birkin bag hung from the fold of her right arm. The fat white diamonds in her earlobes looked like they might have cost twice as much as Markio's necklaces. She had a body that was similar to R&B songstress Ashanti's, slim and pretty up top and extra curvy down below, and it was taking every bit of restraint in Markio to keep his hands from wandering south.

"I've never been to this hotel," she said as they entered the enormous building. "I've been to the Drake Hotel down the street from here, but never the Four Seasons. I had no idea it was so nice and big."

Her eyes were everywhere—checking out the high-class attire of passing guests, the unique red-and-black uniforms worn by the hotel staff, the Italian marble flooring and huge rounded pillars—but Markio's eyes were stuck on her.

What do you really do for a living?" Nikkia asked. "Because according to Terri Pratchett, you work for Johnson Brothers Roofing, and unless you've been contracted to work on Elon Musk's California mega mansion, I don't see you being able to afford this level of luxury."

"I fell into some money," Markio said, raising their interlaced hands to plant a gentle kiss on the back of hers. "Speaking of which, I got a question to ask you about this money."

"Ask away." She gave him a side-eye. "But that'll put me back on the clock, and my standard rate is eight hundred and fifty dollars an hour."

"I bought a storage—Wait, what? Eight hundred and fifty dollars an hour? You for real?"

"Of course, I'm for real. This kind of legal expertise does not come cheap. I've charged some companies $1,350 an hour. Not to mention the thirty-five percent I get from every lawsuit I win. What did you think I charged? I'm the real deal. I've never lost a case, whether it be criminal or civil. I am her. You better *Google* me."

Markio laughed at her undoubtedly well earned cockiness as they got in the elevator. He told the hotel employee waiting inside the elevator which floor they were headed to, and the staff member pressed the button, while Nikkia replied to an email she just received.

Markio took advantage of the quiet elevator ride to read his own new text messages, the first of which was from D-Dot, a guy he used to be somewhat sociable with years ago in Lakeland Project. D-Dot had bought a quarter-pound of gelato weed from him earlier this week, and he was only texting to say his older brother Waddell needed to holler at Markio about something. Another text was from Sway Swanson and that one had just one word: "Fineto."

They got off the elevator and Markio led the way into the romantic honeymoon suite, which was only one floor below his penthouse suite and nearly just as spacious. Together they walked to the huge floor-to-ceiling window overlooking Lake Michigan and gazed out through the vertical blinds.

"So, what's the question?" Nikkia asked, scissoring her thick legs and turning her head to look at him. "I told you to ask away. I love billing people."

"Let's say I went to a storage auction, and I bidded on a particular locker and won it. And when I opened one of the suitcases I got out of that locker I found it packed full of cash. How would I go about dealing with that? Legally, I mean."

"You'd have to report the money to the IRS but it would be yours." She paused, thinking then added, "Well, unless it was stolen property. Like from a bank robbery or something like that. Then it could be seized for evidence and eventually returned to its rightful owner."

"What if it was drug money?"

Nikkia stared at him, her eyes asquint in thought. "Hm. That's a tough one. I mean, if they didn't know it was drug money, I suppose they couldn't seize it. How much money are we talking here. Because the amount would be the ultimate deciding factor in whether or not an investigation is launched."

"It's five million dollars."

Nikkia's lashy eyelids widened in shock. "You found five million dollars in a storage locker?"

Markio answered with a simple nod as he turned and crossed the floor to the bedroom doorway. He looked in at the large heart-shaped bed. It was draped in blood-red linens. Rose petals were sprinkled across the heavy blanket and all over the floor. There were dozens of candles, unlit in their glass holders. A sex swing hung from the ceiling in one corner of the room near a shelf line with books that offered hundreds of new and unique sexual positions.

Out of the corner of his eye Markio watched Nikkia raise the rose to her nose again as she walked toward him. He could see the smile on her face without even looking directly at her. She looked happy, content, genuinely at ease in his company.

He went to the champagne bucket and lifted out the gold bottle of Ace as Nikkia walked in behind him. She took a moment to look around the room and laughed at the sex swing while Markio filled two champagne glasses and brought them over to her.

"They went a little too far with the sex swing," Nikkia said. She accepted the champagne glass and clinked it against Markio's before raising it to her pretty lips. "To us."

"To us," Markio echoed. He turned up the glass and drank down the champagne in three long gulps, his gaze never straying from Nikkia's wet looking lips.

"You're the luckiest man I've ever met." Nikkia set down her bouquet of roses and stepped out of her heels. "You've been saved from a bullet by a pile of cash and you found five million dollars in a locker at a storage auction. I don't think you could possibly get any luckier."

"I already did," he said and closed his muscular arms around her waist. "I found you."

Nikkia rolled her eyes, and her face glowed with joy. Markio's hands were finally able to explore her bountiful derriere, and he wasted no time in doing so, rubbing and squeezing and smacking on her big soft ass as he pressed his lips firmly against hers.

"I'm about to fuck the dog shit outta you," he said, and chuckled.

"Good," she said, "I need it."

***

"...And all of a sudden Lil' Mark pulled the gun on your brother," Mya was saying to Mariah. "I reached down into my purse and searched around for the handle of that big-ass gun, and as soon as I got my hand around the handle I shot him straight through my purse."

There was a collective gasp from the Earl women. They were all gathered together in a circle, each of them with a drink in hand, neither of them paying any mind to the raucous shouts of Rose and her three brothers as they played a game of Spades in the next room. Mariah and Shakia were especially tuned in to Mya's account of last night's shooting. Kayshawna was the only girl who remembered Mya from the neighborhood. The rest of the Earl girls were older, in their mid-to-late thirties, and hadn't spent much time in the streets of North Lawndale in years.

"He shot your brother in the leg," Mya said, looking at Shakia, now a short pretty girl who looked like she could be Markio's twin. "But the crazy thing is Markio had so much money in his pocket that the bullet didn't even go all the way through."

"Whaaat?" Tinky exclaimed. She was a cute chocolate girl with slanted eyes like an Asian, dressed in a Burberry blouse over blue jeans and Nike Air Max 97s.

"I swear on my daddy's grave," Mya went on. "I know it probably sounds too wild to be true, but it's the truth. That's literally what went down. And now I'm beefin' with Lil' Mark's people on Facebook. I just had to block both of his sisters and four of his cousins on IG. The shit is just crazy. I about had a nervous breakdown when my sister called me saying Lil' Mark didn't make it. That's why I had Markio come and pick me up from my girl Nissa's house. I had to get the fuck away for a while. I couldn't take it."

Chanel—a slim albino girl with a sexy figure and eyes that never stopped moving from left to right in their sockets—shook her head and sipped from her cup. "And all this shit happened because my cousin bought Worm's storage locker?"

Shakia said, "Worm was dumb for puttin' all that money in there from jump. Who in their right mind would put five million dollars in a storage locker? Come on, now I know that's your big brother and all, but he was dumb as hell for that one."

"I know. That's why I sided with Markio. Worm made a dumb decision and it cost him a fortune. He can't be mad at Markio about it when Markio was in a whole nother state livin' his best life, and just happened to end being at that auction."

Mya was only drunk-talking now. In truth, she loved her big brother Worm, and she didn't think he was stupid at all. Stashing his money away in that storage locker until he could get himself situated in Indiana had been a good idea, but Mya wasn't about to say it to the five young women standing all around her. Not when they were all related to Markio. His sister Shakia had a reputation for beating bitches down, and Mya wasn't trying to be her next victim.

Mya excused herself to the bathroom when the topic changed to what everyone was going to buy with the cash Markio had given them. She shut and locked the bathroom door and sat down to pee.

"Then she flushed the toilet, washed and dried her hands and *FaceTimed* Worm.

She could see that Worm was seated on the sofa in his basement apartment at their grandmother's Trumbull Avenue building. He looked distraught. Upset. Defeated.

"Your favorite rapper Lil' Durk gon be mad," he said.

"What? Why you say that?"

"Some niggas came through 64th and Normal earlier and sprayed that bitch up. Killed one of his lil' homies. They hit up O-Block, too. I just did some business with Chops, one of Durk's guys, and he say they just put a stupid bag on some nigga named Leezo, or some'n like that—Leezo and Wooski. Guess he think they did it."

"I'm so drunk right now," Mya said, flipping down the toilet lid and plopping down on top of it. She felt a splash of vomit rising up into her throat and grimaced as she swallowed it.

"Where you at?" Worm asked.

"Downtown at the Four Seasons. It's on Delaware, right off Michigan Avenue."

"What the hell you doin' back in Chicago?"

"I'm here with Markio and his people—well, not Markio, he left out a lil' while ago, but all his people still here. His lil' sisters— Mariah and Shakia. Huey, Kay and Buck. A bunch of other cousins.

He passed out money to everybody in there. Big stupid-ass stacks of money."

A burning rage flashed in Big Worm's eyes. He kept his mouth shut and stared at Mya.

"Why you didn't tell me it was five million dollars?" she asked.

"It wasn't none of your business. I keep certain shit from you to keep you safe."

"Well," Mya said snappishly, "why you offer me a million dollars to help you find it if it wasn't none of my business?" She didn't give him time to reply. "And by the way, I know where your money at. But that ain't none of my business so I'll just keep it to myself."

"Don't play with me like that, Mya. If you know where my shit at, tell me."

"She scowled at him for a long moment. She'd give him the info, but she'd make him squirm first.

"Mya!" he yelled, agitated. "Do you know where that nigga got my money at? Yes or no?"

"I just told you I know where he's hiding it."

"Then where the fuck is it?!"

Mya sighed, letting out some of her anger in the exhalation. "It's at his sister Taquisha's house in Michigan City. I saw him go in there with twin empty Louis Vuitton duffle bags before he picked me up, and when he came back out he had those same two duffel bags but I could tell they were heavy. I was watching from Nissa's living room window. You know she stays right next door to Taquisha."

"How do you know the bags had cash in 'em? It could've been clothes or some'n."

"I know because he opened one of the duffle bags when we got here and handed out cash to everybody. Even gave me twenty-five thousand. He got two Nike duffel bags full of cash and twin Louis Vuitton duffle bags full of cash. He took 'em with him when he left out. I think he got another room somewhere in this big-ass hotel, because his lawyer's supposed to be meeting him here. I think he's fucking her too."

Big Worm muttered something under his breath. Then he said something under his breath. Then he said, "I ain't gon' be able to use the Lords this time. Bam ain't gon' send 'em, and you know he the only nigga they'll listen to."

"What? Why won't he send 'em? He don't wanna help you find your money?"

"Nah. He feel like Kio was in the right, and he say we done already sacrificed Ace and Lil' Mark. He gotta pay for their funerals. He had to bond out the other boys who got arrested out there. Baby Lord still in the hospital out there, and they got him handcuffed to the bed, under arrest. Pee Wee locked up out here with no bond. I understood Bam's position, but fuck that. I want my money. If he won't help me get it, I'll just have to find a way to get it myself." He paused, then added, "I'ma have to send Lil' Worm. Hold on. I'm about to join him on this *FaceTime* call."

***

Nikkia had told her assistant to fetch her an outfit and some other things from her home, and while she waited she'd taken a soak in the candle-lined bathtub while Markio smoked a blunt of gelato and made two phone calls; one to Reggie and the other to his nephew—Tyquan.

It was Markio who went to the door to get Nikkia's things from the assistant, a dark-hued, nerdy-looking young woman wearing white-framed eyeglasses and a yellow pantsuit. She handed Markio the handle of a rolling Gucci suitcase, said thank you, and walked awkwardly away.

Markio rolled the suitcase up to the bathroom door and Nikkia opened the door just long enough to snatch the suitcase inside—just long enough for Markio to get a good look at her beautiful naked body, wet and dripping, her hair thrown up in a messy topknot. Her titties were perfectly perky, her abdomen tight and flat, and there wasn't a trace of hair on her pussy. The way her hips spread out below her waist made Markio's mouth water.

"Come on out here," he said pleadingly.

"Greatness takes time. Haven't you heard that? Five more minutes."

She shut the door, and Markio fell against it, his dick growing longer and harder by the second. He'd been ready to fuck Nikkia the moment they entered the honeymoon suite, and she'd made him wait for her to take a bath, and for her assistant to arrive, and now he had to wait five more minutes? There was a word for the inhumane way she was treating him: *torture.*

"I'm dyin' out here," he said, knocking his forehead against the door.

"I'll revive you in five minutes," Nikkia replied smartly.

Markio went to the bookshelf, picked up a book titled *Kama Sutra*, and flipped through the pages, marveling at some of the interesting and not-so-interesting positions. He decided he'd try a few of them. He didn't have anything to lose. He had a big dick, as he was sure it would feel good to Nikkia no matter how strange the position.

He didn't have long to wait. The bathroom door opened, and Nikkia stood in the doorway with her hands on her hips, wearing nothing but a thin layer of make-up—foundation, pink lip gloss, and eye shadow. She was a paragon of African American female beauty, the epitome of black girl magic, and Markio knew right then that he had found his Beyonce, his Alexus Castilla. Nikkia possessed the kind of unmatched pulchritude that didn't need make-up in the morning for a man to want to stick around forever, which was exactly what Markio wanted to do.

"I'm telling you now," she said, sauntering toward him, "I'm not a big fan of the whole dick sucking thing. I'll do it, but I'm just not that into it. Don't get me wrong, I love getting head—oh, gawd, how I love getting head—but I'm not too fond of giving it."

"That's fine with me. I'll take whatever I can get."

Nikkia folded her arms around his neck, and they kissed for some time. Her breath was fresh and sweet, like her perfume. He groped her meaty derriere, then slipped one hand around between them and began to fiercely rub his fingertips against her clitoris. The harder he rubbed, the hungrier her kisses became, and soon she was sticking her tongue deep in his mouth, moaning and panting.

The moment Nikkia seized up and yelped out a high pitched moan caught Markio by surprise. He kept rubbing as her body trembled and shook against him, a smile stretching across his face as he realized what he'd just done to her.

"Damn, you came already?" he asked with an amused grin.

Nikkia was still trembling as she shoved away from him, smiling and panting with her mouth wide open. "I—told you—it's been a while," she said, walking to the bed on shaky legs and falling forward across it. Her ass and thighs wobbled like Jello as she landed.

Markio was on her in an instant, spreading her fat butt cheeks apart and lapping up the escaping vaginal nectar from between her thick labia. She tasted wonderfully delicious, like some never-released treat straight out of Willy Wonka's Chocolate Factory. She found the strength to pull herself up onto her knees, separating them as Markio slipped his head in between them and rolled over onto his back.

"Yass," Nikkia said, lowering her pussy onto his eagerly awaiting mouth. Markio could see the joyful smile on her sexy caramel brown face as she did it, a smile that quickly morphed into an expression of pure ecstasy as he began to lick and suck on her fat pussy lips, pushing back a little to get at her clit before going back to slaking his thirst with her plentiful inner juices.

She rode his face for a while, tweaking her erect nipples between her thumbs and fingers, tossing her head back and moaning. The sight of it all had Markio's dick ready to bust out of his jeans. He held on to her thighs, pulling her down on his mouth and drawing himself in the best tasting pussy he'd ever eaten.

Nikkia trembled her way through a second orgasm not even five minutes later, shivering and jerking around on Markio's face. Her juices trickled out from between her wet, quivering labia and dripped down onto his tongue, and she let out a long, low moan.

"Stop-stop-stop," she said, smacking him on the top of his head.

Markio released his iron grip on her thighs, and she fell over next to him, her chest rising and falling as she stared up at the ceiling and laughed out loud.

"Turn on some music," she said breathlessly, "and take off that shirt and those jeans. Let me see that dick."

Markio was more than happy to oblige. He connected his iPhone to the charger and pressed play on his R&B playlist. He'd already figured out how to use the suite's Bluetooth speakers, and seconds later the room filled with the romantic ballad of Chris Brown's "Privacy" as Markio took off his shoes, then his shirt, and finally his expensive designer jeans.

Nikkia sat up in bed and stared impatiently at the huge erection in his Louis Vuitton boxer briefs. "Why'd you change clothes again?" she asked. "The Louis Vuitton outfit you wore to lunch was fly as hell. This is the third outfit I've seen you in today."

"I think I might've got some gunpowder on that Louis Vuitton fit. Had to switch it out," Markio said, ripping open the gold wrapper of a Magnum condom and tossing the wrapper aside.

"I believe you really did that. Crazy ass." Nikkia pointed at his underwear. "Lose those, too."

"Damn. Lil' Thirsty," Markio joked, but he wasted no time in honoring her request, losing the boxer-briefs in a hurry and then climbing up onto the bed on his knees.

"Ooouuu, you got a pretty dick," Nikkia said, taking hold of it before Markio could roll the condom on. "And it's so long. You know what? I might actually like sucking on this. I might have to change my position on fellatio."

"Shut up and lay back." Markio palmed her face in his hand and pushed, and she fell back, snickering sweetly. The large Magnum condom fit snugly around his dick. He rubbed the head up and down between her vaginal lips and then eased it in.

The warmth of her slippery inner muscles clenching tightly around the condom as he sank into her made Markio inhale sharply, filling his lungs to capacity. He went in and out a couple of times then lifted one of her legs onto his shoulder and started penetrating her at an angle, looking up at the open-mouthed expression frozen on her impossibly sexy face.

"You done fucked up," he said. "You done fucked all the way up. You cain't give a real nigga like me no pussy. I just popped two Perc thirties. I'ma fuck you all night."

Nikkia was in no position to reply. Her eyes flicked over to look at him, but her mouth remained open as he pounded in and out of her. She may not have been able to fix her lips to speak, but the glazed-over look in her eyes spoke volumes. She was in a state of absolute bliss.

Markio leaned down to kiss her on the chin. Then he cupped her left titty in his right hand sucked the hard nipple into his mouth and rolled his tongue around it as he continued to fuck her senseless.

Chapter Twelve

Baby Lord was wide awake in the hospital room, staring at the television suspended from the ceiling between the two beds without really watching the show that was on it. His vision was blurred by the tears in his eyes, and he only had one hand to wipe them away, because his left wrist was handcuffed to the bedrail. He'd been wiping away the tears all day, but they wouldn't stop coming. His cousin Ace was dead, shot in the face by some bitch named Whitney Clarrett, and since Ace was killed while he and Baby Lord were attempting to kidnap Whitney Clarrett, Baby Lord was being charged with his own cousin's murder.

There was a cop sitting just outside the door to his hospital room waiting for the doctor's okay to transport him to the local county jail—wherever the hell that was.

The short, dark-skinned young black man in the other bed had yet to awaken. Baby Lord had overheard Star, the sexy chocolate nurse who'd drawn his blood a few hours earlier, saying that the young man had suffered two gunshot wounds in a shooting a few hours ago, and they'd put him on heavy pain meds. Baby Lord had taken a bullet to the upper left side of his chest, and the medication dripping into his IV had him feeling numb and relaxed, but it did little to alleviate the emotional ache.

The time was 7:08 p.m. when the other young man stirred in bed and opened his eyes. He looked around, confused, then slowly turned his head in Baby Lord's direction and opened his mouth to speak. It took a few seconds for the words to come out.

"Folks n'em left me," he muttered, his eyes darting around again.

The phrase 'Folks *n'em*' made Baby Lord's eyes widen in surprise. That was a Chicago phrase. That and the young man's nasal accent led Baby Lord to further believe he was in the presence of a fellow Chicagoan. He blinked the tears out of his eyes to give his roommate a closer look.

"You from the Raq?" Baby Lord asked, meaning Chiragz—a nickname given to Chicago years ago by some Sun Times journalist who'd compared Chicago murder rate to the terrorist-ridded country of Iraq.

The man nodded weakly. "Englewood, you?"

"I'm from out west. Chicago Avenue and Trumbull. My name Ikey, but everybody call me Baby Lord. What hood you from in Englewood?"

"63rd and St. Lawrence." The young man chuckled dryly. "My name Ikey, too."

"Ha! Hell naw." Baby Lord buzzed the head of his bed upward. "What, you a BD?"

"Man, don't disrespect me like that," Ikey said groggily. "I'm a GD, fam. From Tookaville. Getcha shit splat Gang. All we do is lamp on the BDs and slam they ass when we catch em." He shifted around in the bed, winced at an ache, and said, "We came out here to nail some hoe ass nigga, and I got hit up on the drill. Folks n'em left me bleedin' in front of the hospital. Thought I was gon' die."

"We come out here on damn near the same shit," Baby Lord said. "We tried to snatch up this bad bitch for one of the big homies and didn't know she had a pipe on her. She upped that bitch. Shot my cousin in the face, then shot up the whip we was in. Hit me in the chest. They chargin' me for my cousin's murder 'cause it happened while we was tryna kidnap that bitch. Shit crazy." Baby Lord wiped the wet streaks from his dark-hued face. "And we still ain't find that five million."

"Yeah, my big homie Worm and his brother Bam got bricks, and Worm big dumb-ass hid five M's in a storage locker out here. He got shot up and put in a coma, and when he came out the coma they had already auctioned the locker off. Some bitch named Whitney Clarrett ended up with it. We tried to kidnap her and she whacked cuzzo and blew at us."

"I bet she did," Ikey said, the grogginess leaving his voice the more he spoke. "If I had five M's, I wouldn't be playin' about it, either. I'll do like Rooga did when he got them M's from Kanye. That nigga got the fuck out the hood soon as that check cleared."

"Crazy thing is," Baby Lord said, "that pretty nurse let me use her phone to make a call about a hour ago, and I called Bam. He say the bitch Whitney Clarrett didn't even have the money. He say this nigga named Markio had it the whole time. So we was goin' after the wrong person and didn't even know it."

Ikey gasped. "Get the fuck outta here. Markio? Man, that's who we just blew down. On fo'nem grave, shorty bum-ass just got his whole shit pushed back."

"Nah," Baby Lord said, shaking his head stiffly; too much movement would upset the bullet wound in his chest. "Markio ain't dead. You was right here asleep when I made the call, and Worm had just talked to Markio. Plus, one of Markio's lil' sisters had just gone live on the Gram at some hotel party, and Markio was in the background of the video. Bam say he had on a white Givenchy shirt, Amiri jeans. Say he had some ice on his neck. He definitely ain't dead, and he definitely got that five million."

A look of utter confusion swept across Ikey's face. It was clear that he had more questions to ask, but he wouldn't get the chance to ask them. Just then, the door to their room was pushed open, and three uniformed police officers entered the room, one of them pushing an empty wheelchair.

"Okay, Mr. Williams," one officer said to Baby Lord. "It's time for you to come with us. And don't worry, the beds in the county jail infirmary are just as comfortable as these."

The three cops laughed heartily. They prepared Baby Lord to be transported to the Laporte County Jail, shackling his ankles and wrapping a chain around his waist to attach the handcuffs to, and as they wheeled him out of the room, he glanced over at Ikey and saw that the look of confusion was still there. Through the fog of pain meds, Ikey was slowly beginning to realize that he and his gang had murdered the wrong man, and that the right man was sitting on $5 million.

***

"Listen, Dame," Mulberry said, her ominous tone of voice conveying the severity of the situation. "You need to be very careful going after this guy, all right? There's some seriously dangerous things going on in this city, and Markio Earl is smack-dab in the middle of it."

"I ain't worried about that dude," Dame replied, steering his Grand Cherokee into the McDonald's parking lot and pulling in beside a dark red Honda Accord. "Markio ain't nobody. He might have all these other niggas out here scared, but that trigger-happy hit don't move me none. He just another soft-ass wannabe gangsta, too scared of takin' a L to knuckle up, so all he do is shoot people."

"No, Dame. You don't understand," Mulberry explained. "You see, when I turned you loose on Markio Earl, I also put a few other guys on him. So there were four of you altogether. Two of them have been killed within the last couple of hours, one shot to death in Lakeland, the other killed in an intentional hit-and-run after leaving a barber shop on Michigan Boulevard. Now, I don't believe in coincidences. I think Markio knew those guys were informants, and he had them killed for trying to reel him in. I don't need you making that same mistake."

"I won't, Mulberry. I got this. Look, I gotta go. I'll call you back soon's he reply to my message."

He ended the call and muttered a bunch of profanities under his breath. Trina, the transsexual whose wig-covered head was currently bobbing up and down in his lap, didn't miss a beat, slamming his dick to the back of her throat with every downward stroke of the head. Dame had a wife at home, but he'd been creeping around with Trina for about eight months now. His wife was an attractive Puerto Rican woman who couldn't suck a dick the right way if her life depended on it. On the other hand, Brandon "Trina" Arnold—who looked a lot like a real woman, with C-cup breasts and a big fake ass that felt like the real thing—sucked dick like it was what she was born to do. Dame never had to worry about Trina's teeth scraping painfully over the head of his dick, and Trina never shied away from cumshot, unlike his wife, who practically chewed on his dick and treated every cumshot as if it was some venomous fluid spit from the fangs of a hissing King Cobra.

Dame took the AirPods out of his ears and relaxed in his seat, closing his eyes to enjoy the heavenly feel of Trina's tightly sucking mouth gliding up and down his seven-inch erection.

"That's it," he whispered. "Eat that dick, girl. Eat that dick just like that."

He dropped his head back against the headrest. Flexed his toes in his work boots. Inhaled and exhaled and did it again, focusing on his breathing. He felt warm saliva oozing down his balls. Heard the wet, slashing sounds of Trina's saliva-drenched mouth slurping him to a soul-shaking climax. He tried holding back a moment longer but it was no use. Trina's head was just too good. He shot off into the tranny's steadily sucking mouth.

Markio Earl and the so-called danger he posed were the furthest thing from Dame's mind.

That was until the rear driver's side door behind him swung open, and a man wearing a black hoodie and a matching ski-mask climbed in to join him and Trina in his SUV.

The man put a gun to the side of Dame's neck, and Trina calmly lifted her head from his lap, as if the gunman were a figment of Dame's imagination.

"Drive, bitch," Trina said, and when Dame turned to look at her, she spit the semen she'd just caught in her mouth all over his face. "Down Carroll Ave to the train station. Let's go."

"Yeah," said the man in the seat behind Dame. "Let's go. Rat-ass nigga."

***

Whitney and Flocka were walking out of McDonald's, heading toward her dark red Honda Accord, when a blue Buick Roadmaster with a damaged front end sped into the parking lot and stopped behind the snot-green Jeep that had parked next to her Honda. A tall man wearing a black hoodie and a ski-mask emerged from the passenger's side of the Roadmaster and jumped into the back of the Jeep, and the Roadmaster pulled off in a hurry.

"Whoa, whoa. Stop," Whitney said. She stepped back, and Flocka did the same, watching as the Jeep backed out of the parking space and turned to leave. She caught a brief glimpse of the Jeep's driver—he looked like he might be handsome, but there was a thick white slime dripping down the front of his face—and she recognized his passenger as Trina, a tranny she'd known since he was just a feminine little boy. Then the Jeep drove out of the parking lot, making a left onto Carroll Avenue and disappearing down the street.

Whitney stopped to look around. A white girl who'd just stepped out of a Ford Focus was already on her phone with the police. She seemed to be the only other eyewitness to the crime.

"Fuck this shit. Get in the car," Whitney said.

She and Flocka rushed to her Honda and got in, and she drove off fast, wanting nothing to do with the police when they arrived. She'd seen enough of the Michigan City Police Department yesterday alone to last a lifetime and she'd just picked up Flocka from the McDonald's after the police had freed him from custody not even a half an hour ago.

"Okay," she said, when they were a full six blocks away from the McDonald's. "From start to finish. Tell me everything. Including whatever you told the police, because I seriously wanna know how you got out so fast, with no bond or nothin'."

"I blamed it all on Mellie Mel," Flocka said. "He dead anyway, so I figured I might as well put the break-in on him. I told the detectives Mellie Mel called me and told me to meet him at his cousin's house on Vail Street, and I didn't know he had kicked the door in until I walked in the kitchen and saw the wood splinters on the floor. Then them niggas popped up on the back porch as we was leavin' and shot bro in the head, so I shot back and ran. Hurt my ankle jumpin' off the front porch, but I'm good. They kept my gun for *investigative purposes*, whatever the fuck that means, but they knew I didn't kill bro 'cause all the gun shells on the back porch came from rifles. So they had to let me go. I saw Rica G ridin' past and flagged him down, had him drop me off at the McDonald's so I could put some'n in my stomach. That's when I called you."

Whitney weighed his story on her mental scale of truth and decided she believed him. "What about the suitcases?" she asked. "Eight big steel suitcases. Did you see them?"

"Nope. We went through that whole house. Ain't a suitcase to be seen." Flocka gave her a hard look. "I need some money. I know I didn't earn the fifty racks, but I feel like—"

"Calm down. I got five thousand for you. Just keep your mouth shut about what happened today. Don't tell my kids anything about this. Jimmy's already crying like a baby over Mellie, and his sisters are sad for him, so I got four sad teenagers in my house, and the last thing I need is for them to find out that their mama was behind the whole thing."

"What about Markio? He gon' find out it was me and Mellie Mel who broke in his house. The police report'll tell him that much. It'll be in the newspaper tomorrow."

"I know." Whitney sighed. There was no easy answer to that one. Markio had the money, and she'd fucked up royally by sending her son's two best friends to break into his house. "Let me worry about that," she said with another hopeless sigh. "Just keep your lips sealed. If Jimmy asks, tell him the same story you told the police."

Whitney drove Flocka to Coolspring Apartments and gave him the five grand from her new Chanel bag before she let him out. She'd separated it from the bundle of cash beforehand, to keep him from being tempted to snatch the entire fifty thousand dollars. He pocketed the pile of hundreds and tried to kiss her on the mouth, but she turned her head at the last second and his lips grazed her cheek.

He hesitated, looking at her, and as luck would have it her phone rang at that very moment. Flocka pushed open his door and got out as she answered the call. It was from an unfamiliar number with a 773 area code. Flocka slammed the door unnecessarily hard and limped off. Whitney waited until she had backed out and drove away to speak.

"Hello? Who is this?"

"Is this Whitney Clarrett?" It was a woman's voice, soft and sweet.

"Yes, it is. Now who am I talking to? I don't have your number saved in my phone."

"We kinda got off on the wrong foot yesterday. I'm Yasmine Gordon, but everybody calls me Bunny. I'm the girl you and your daughter jumped in the hospital parking lot."

Whitney laughed. "Oh, okay. Sorry about that. I mean, you deserved it for following me and watching my house, but still I thought G-Money had sent you."

"Yeah, I shouldn't have followed you. And if you're wondering how I got your name, address, and phone number blame it on the front desk lady at Michiana Storage Masters. She gave it to me. But listen: I heard you tell your kids to have Markio check the suitcases, and I'm pretty sure he found millions of dollars when he opened them. And if he's like most men I know, he probably didn't cut you in like you hoped he would. Am I right so far?"

"Keep going," Whitney said.

"That money's chump change," Bunny continued. "the man it belonged to is one of my side niggas, and he blows way more than he saves. He's probably already made another million dollars since he lost that money. But forget him. He's a small fish. Right now I'm laid out next to an Infinity pool behind one of the largest mansions in Miami Beach. It's Keondre Muck's summer home, and yes I do mean the same Keondre Muck who just signed to the Denver Broncos for two hundred and ten million. He's got three teammates staying here with him until Monday morning and they're all young black millionaires. A bad bitch like you can come down here and snag one of these rich niggas in a heartbeat. I'll have Keondre pay for a first-class ticket that'll have you here tonight."

Whitney's brow rose in anticipation of such a rare opportunity, but a part of her remained skeptical. "And why would you do something like that for me, the woman who beat your ass yesterday? Explain that to me. Why would you wanna help?"

"I don't know. I have a good heart. And Bam told me about you killing one of his younger gang members in self-defense, and about them ransacking your place. I feel bad because they wouldn't have known anything about you had I not gone to the storage place and paid that lady for your information. I was wrong, and this is my way of making it right." She went silent for a couple of seconds' then, in a slightly less confident tone of voice, she added, "Plus, you know, I don't have a lot of female friends. I'm a porn actress, and a lot of girls aren't too comfortable with that. They either think I'm gonna fuck their men or their men think I'm gonna have their girlfriends doing porn. That's why a lot of us in the porn industry date each other. But enough about me. You coming or not?"

Whitney had already pulled over next to Joy Elementary School and *Googled* 'Yasmine Bunny,' and now she was looking at Yasmine. "BunnyXXX" Gordon's social media profiles as she spoke with the porn star on the phone. The girl was telling the truth. She had millions of followers on every major social media platform. Whitney tapped on a Pornhub link and realized she'd already seen a few of BunnyXXX's famous blowjob videos.

"Wow. You're the porn star they call the Throat Goat," Whitney murmured in disbelief.

"That's me. BunnyXXX. You can just call me Bunny, though. I gotta go; my manager's calling me on the other line. Text me if you want that first-class ticket. You won't regret it, I promise."

The call came to an end, and Whitney breathed in deep and let it all out, deflating her lungs completely. The whole first-class-ticket-to-paradise thing sounded too good to be true, but her instinct told her to believe it. And after all the bullshit she'd gone through since yesterday, a vacation was exactly what she needed, especially if it included hanging out with four millionaire NFL players.

After a long moment of intense contemplation Whitney composed a text message to Bunny" '*Okay, I'm in. Send the ticket.*'

Chapter Thirteen

"Oh, my God, Markio. Oh—my—gawd!" Nikkia screamed in between moans, burying her face in a fluffy, silk encased pillow, the center of her back rising like a frightened feline's as she experienced her fifth orgasm of the evening.

Markio put his hand on the middle of her back and pushed down, forcing it back into the sexy arch he'd been looking at for the past twenty-something minutes. His pistoning dick was coated from end to end with her bubble white cream, and he had his thumb in her pretty little but hole as he continued his relentless assault on her pussy.

The glowing red numbers on the bedside digital clock read 8:27 p.m. which meant Markio had been digging in Nikkia for exactly one hour and fifty-two minutes. He had stopped twice, to suck and lick and blow on her clitoris for a few minutes and bring her orgasm, and then he'd continued on dicking her down. He couldn't remember ever fucking a woman for so long, and when he snatched off the condom a few minutes later and shot thick ropes of cum all over her ass and lower back, it was an overflow of semen, more than he'd ever ejaculated at once.

He shivered, squeezing out the last few drops of it and then paused to admire the mess he'd made. Nikkia looked back at it, snickering shakily, and repeated the phrase that had become her own litter mantra over the past two hours.

"Oh, my gawd," she said. "What the hell? Go in there and get me a towel to wipe off all this gunk. How did your balls even hold all that? Why didn't you just put it in the condom?"

Markio had no words. He tumbled onto his back and lay there panting, worn-out and suddenly very sleepy. His playlist had progressed to a list of hits by Kodak Black, and one of his favorite songs of the moment, "Killing The Rats," was currently playing:

She callin' me Yak, yeah, baby, do it like that, I like when it snatch
I'm smokin' the roach, and killin' the rats

Smokin' the roach, and I'm killin' the rats
When I'm back in the jets I be flippin' the pack
Smokin' the roach, and killin' the rats
Everythin' I got, I took, and if I owed ya, bitch, I paid ya
back
Her face in my lap, I'm grippin' the strap

Nikkia sucked her teeth as Markio closed his eyes beside her, but when he peeked over at her five seconds later she was smiling—glowing, like the numbers on the bedside clock—and crawling backwards on her hands and knees to keep his cum from soiling the plush red blanket. There were two rose petals stuck to her skin, one on the side of her neck and another on her left titty, right on the nipple. She had a large rose tatted on her left hip. Her thick butt cheeks bounced and jiggled as she walked to the adjoining bathroom, with two strings of translucent white goo stretching down from her left buttock like hot cheese on a pizza.

Markio sat up to put on his boxer-briefs and looked over the side of the bed to make sure that one of the four duffel bags he'd placed there was still open, the butt of his Draco sticking up out of the mountain of cash the duffel contained. Then he laid back, closed his eyes again, and finished listening to the Kodak Black song, suddenly realizing that he'd started living out the song title without even thinking about it, literally killing the rats the police were sending at him—or at least having them killed.

The last thing he remembered before drifting off was the sound of the shower turning on in the bathroom and Nikkia yelling out, "Who puts Kodak Black on their R & B playlist? Like, for real."

A gangsta-ass nigga like me, Markio thought, but he was too tired to say it, and a second later he was fast asleep. Though not for long.

Any hopes of getting a full night's sleep were dashed when Nikkia climbed on top of him an hour later, awakening him from a dreamless rest. She was dressed in a black leather shirt, a green Chanel blouse, and diamond Chanel earrings, and she had his iPhone in her hand. She turned the screen toward his face and used the facial recognition feature to unlock the screen.

"Get up," she said, and leaned down to kiss him on the lips. "I let you sleep for an hour, and your phone's been ringing the whole time. That's what woke me up."

She began scrolling through his missed calls while he rubbed his hands back and forth on her smooth brown thighs. He didn't have anything to hide in his phone. He'd already deleted the entire thread of messages between him and Whitney and blocked her number from his phone, and Nikkia already knew about Mya. Aside from that, the rest of his contacts were mostly family and friends.

"Who is Mariah?" Nikkia asked.

"That's one of my lil' sisters. She upstairs in the penthouse suite with everybody else."

"Not according to this text she sent at 8:53 p.m. It says, "Not sure where you went, but I'm heading home to be with Marleigh and Jam. Thanks for the money, big brother." You got seven missed calls from Reggie, Fat Jerm, Sway, Cocky Lord, Buck, D-Dot, and Tyquan. And you got three more new text messages. Want me to read 'em to you?"

Markio smirked and gave her a light smack on the thigh, taking her free hand in his and planting a kiss on the back of it. "You can read to me for the rest of my life," he said.

Nikkia rolled her eyes and looked down her slender nose at him. "Okay, you can stop tryin' so hard now," she said through a cheesy smile. "You already got the goodies. Heck, I think you might've broken the goodies. I can hardly even walk straight. My kitty is actually swollen right now."

"Yeah? Let me rub it and make it better." He reached in between her thighs and received a sharp smack on the forearm for the transgression, exactly on the stitched-up face of his Chucky doll tattoo. He snatched back and rubbed the stinging spot on his forearm.

"So, Nikkia went on, "The first text is from Tyquan, and it reads, '*Got that from Goldmouth, unc. Thanks. We ready for em*'. Not sure if I even wanna know what that means. The next text is from Reggie and he says, '*Just handled that. On my way now.*' And the last one is from D-Dot, and it says, '*Waddell said call him when you get a chance, here go his number.*' He left Waddell's number, too." Her smile brightened. "And now on to your social media. Don't worry, I won't pry. Just gonna follow myself so I can follow you back. If you've got any pictures or videos of your exes in there, delete them at your earliest convenience."

Markio was liking this bossy side of Nikkia. He'd never let her or anyone else walk all over him but as the saying went, happy wife, happy life, and since Nikkia was the definition of wifey material, he had no problem with letting her control the narrative.

He got dressed and picked up the Louis Vuitton duffle bag that held his Draco, zipping it shut. He had $250,000 in hundred-dollar bills in the duffel, as well as his Ruger pistol and almost three ounces of gelato weed hidden beneath the bundles of cash.

Watching Nikkia as she stood at one of the many wall-mounted mirrors, applying a second coat of gloss to her lips, Markio began to have second thoughts. He wondered what a successful attorney like Nikkia Staples—a partner in one of the most powerful law firms in the Midwest, a woman with ties to Alexus Castilla, whose $294 billion net worth made her the second wealthiest person on earth—could possibly see in a convicted felon like him. But he didn't dare ask, for fear that the answer would do him more harm than good, so instead he went to the mirror next to the one she was using and took out his iPhone.

Markio hadn't stunted on the Gram in a minute, but right now he was feeling himself. He had on two glistening diamond necklaces, a diamond encrusted five-pointed-star pinkie ring, a rose gold Rolex watch, a fresh white Givenchy shirt over cash-stuffed white Amiri jeans. He unzipped the duffel bag, lifted out a fifty-thousand-dollar bundle of hundreds, and raised his phone, aiming the camera at the mirror in front of him as he went live on Instagram. He didn't say a word, choosing instead to let his appearance and the tall block of cash he was holding in his left hand speak for him.

Nikkia noticed what he was doing and got in on it with him, pulling out her own iPhone and going live on her own IG page. She stepped in front of Markio, posing, throwing her head to the side, grabbing her hip. Her Louboutin booties were green like her Chanel blouse, her large Chanel bag black like her leather skirt.

The fact that Nikkia would reveal that the two of them were in a romantic suite together bolstered Markio's faith in their potential as a couple. The views on his video began to go up rather quickly, with numerous people commenting with heart emojis and side-eye emojis and flame emojis. A few commenters who didn't know Nikkia asked who she was, and a lot of people who did know her posted her name in all caps, shocked that she'd be in a hotel room with the likes of him. He glanced at Nikkia's phone and saw that her views far exceeded his. She was already up to more than eight thousand viewers and counting.

When they ended the videos, Nikkia said, "Bitches are about to be more upset than Drake out here. Every girl you've ever dated in MC knows who I am. I'm the one girl who climbed out of that city and made it big, and now I've somehow managed to get the man I've wanted since third grade." Her eyes and mouth went wide, and she looked up from her phone seemingly to gauge Markio's reaction to her unwitting confession. "Oops, I said too much. Damn you, champagne. That's the reason I limit my drinking. I can't drink and keep a secret to save my life."

So you had a crush on me, too?" Markio smiled wide and hard, jokingly popping his collar as he turned back to the mirror. "I knew you loved me. You can't resist all this handsome-ass player shit I got goin' on over here."

Nikkia rolled her eyes, laughing and shaking her head. "Oh, my God. Please don't start getting a big head. Your head's already big enough. Where are we going? And don't say to anybody's hood, because I look too good to be standing around outside."

"You ain't gotta go home to your kids?" Markio asked, returning the bundle of cash to his duffel. A part of him was hoping for a small amount of alone time tonight. He had to go and meet up with Worm, and he didn't want Nikkia near the potentially volatile meeting.

"No, they're with the ex-hubby and his new fiancée in Athens, Greece. They won't land back in the States until sometime Sunday night."

"We can't go too far," Markio said. "I got my whole family upstairs."

"Then it's upstairs we go. "Nikkia picked up her Chanel bag and sauntered out of the room, with Markio trailing close behind her, struggling to come up with a valid excuse to get away from her long enough to slide on Big Worm.

***

Big Worm couldn't remember a time in all his four decades of living when he'd been more enraged than he was right now. Nothing even came close.

He'd been reclined in a comfortable leather chair, trying to give his aching body a rest while scrolling through social media on his iPad, when he ran across the Instagram live video of Markio and the famous lawyer chick. The Shade Room had reposted the video with the caption, "Looks like Queen A's bestie Nikkia Staples done found her a new boo."

"This hoe-ass nigga," Worm muttered incredulously, a scowl replacing his previously relaxed expression. His nostrils flared. His toes curled over in his Gucci flip-flops.

He studied the video. The diamond necklaces around a neck he wanted to strangle. The white Givenchy shirt on a chest he wanted to fill with holes. The rubber-banded pile of hundreds that belonged to him, not Markio. Even the Louis Vuitton phone case infuriated Worm. Markio was living like a king off his hard-earned drug money. The celebrity attorney was Nikkia Staples, who Worm only knew because he was one of the four hundred million people who followed Alexus Castilla on Instagram, and Nikkia Staples was among the select few who were fortunate that Nikkia's ex-husband had gotten $170 million in the divorce settlement, so Nikkia was likely worth at least that much. Markio could easily return Worm's

$5 million and still live like a boss with a badass rich bitch like Nikkia Staples at his side.

If Markio thought Worm was going to settle for just a few hundred thousand dollars, he was sorely mistaken. Worm had made up his mind. He would get his riches back or die trying.

Worm picked up his iPhone and *FaceTimed* his son Lil' Worm, who answered immediately and panned the camera around the inside of his 2020 Grand Cherokee Trailhawk. His friend and fellow gang member, Jack, a cancer-thin-teenager who'd survived being shot six times last year was driving. His other friend, Mannie, who at 6'8" was the tallest young nigga in the hood, was in the backseat, loading an extended clip with fat .45 caliber bullets.

"I see you, big homie," Mannie said to Big Worm's image on the phone screen.

"Glad to see you out that coma," Jack said, as Lil' Worm brought the camera back to his own face.

"We on the way out there right now, Pops," he said. "Just hit the highway. I'll call you as soon as we make it to the address."

"A'ight," Big Worm said. "And listen: I want you to get the suitcases first, but after that, I want y'all to kill whoever y'all see in there. I don't give a fuck if it's a nine-month old baby or a ninety-year-old woman. Kill everybody in that house."

"But, Pops, I thought you just wanted us to grab the eight suit—
"

"Forget what I said before. This nigga Markio got me fucked up. Think he can just take my shit and splurge all on Instagram, buyin' diamond necklaces and shit. Nah, I ain't goin' for that. Whack whoever in there. I don't care if it's his mama. And don't tell Bam nothin' about it. Your uncle actin' like this nigga Markio in the right or some'n"

Jack said, "Ay, big homie. My daddy say he know Markio from way back when, before I was even born. He say that lil' nigga ain't to be fucked with, say he'll pop out and drop some'n with the quickness. My daddy know some stones from Harvey who was in the joint with Markio, and they say he was a savage in that bitch, butcherin' niggas, whoopin' the guards. On gang, they say shorty with the shit."

"I don't give a fuck what that nigga did in prison! Get me my fuckin' money and kill everything in sight! Don't call me back until it's done!"

Big Worm ended the call in a white-hot rage and threw his phone across the room, gritting his teeth and slamming his fist down hard on the arm of his leather chair. Bam had almost convinced him to let go of his animosity towards Markio and move on, but that was over. After he got his money back, he was going to put $250,000 on Markio's head. And if he didn't get his money back, he would put $500,000 on Markio' head. He'd already contacted Freckles, his Atlanta-based heroin plug, and ordered ten kilos of heroin and ten kilos of fentanyl—half of which he'd pay for up front, the other half on the back end—and he planned to turn that load into seventy kilos. If it came down to it, he was willing to give up to ten of those bricks to whoever put a dozen or more bullets in Markio's head.

Either way, Worm wasn't going to breathe easy until Markio Earl was six feet in the ground.

***

Maria and Hot Rod had left, but Markio's brother Lil' Bill and his girlfriend Poochie were among the nine other family members and close friends who'd arrived at the penthouse suite. Rev. G and Cocky, two OG's from North Lawndale were there. Markio's cousins—Tweety, Bear, and Ernie—were also present, as were Buck's girlfriend: Lana, and the Earl matriarch herself, Miss Carolyn Earl.

All eyes fell on Markio and his date when they walked through the door, most of them more focused on Nikkia than Markio. And he understood why. His phone was already flooded with text messages. His social media pages were lighting up with notifications and inbox messages. Everyone was going crazy over him being with Nikkia. He'd heard about her success as a big-time attorney, but he'd never expected to receive so much attention from a simple Instagram video with her.

"I heard all about that money, nigga," Lil' Bill said as he drunkenly crossed the room with a large bottle of Crown Royal in one hand. "Where my cut? I need my cut."

Bill and Markio looked a lot alike, only Bill was taller and had gone almost completely gray. He was a factory worker, and his girlfriend Poochie was a school teacher. Markio considered checking Bill for being so rude, but he knew it was only the alcohol talking, so he blew it off and turned to the family to introduce Nikkia.

Bill wouldn't let up. He stood right next to Markio and tapped him on the shoulder. Asked for the money again. Bill was a loyal sibling, but he could be an annoying drunk. Markio gave him a sour stare, then said fuck it and dug in the duffel, handing Bill a fifty-thousand-dollar bundle. He gave his Aunt Carolyn $50,000 to split with Lana, and gave Cocky $50,000 to split with Rev. G. He handed the last $100,000 to his big cousin Tweety and told him to split it with Ernie and Bear.

"Don't say I ain't never gave y'all nothing," Markio said, happy to see all the smiles around the room. Cocky Lord handed him a blunt and he took two tokes and passed it on to Rev. G, basking in the excitement of the moment, proud to have given away so much cash to his people today.

He spent the next fifteen minutes keeping track of Nikkia, making sure she was comfortable while she mingled with the girls, each of whom had a hundred questions about Alexus Castilla.

Finally, after smoking a blunt with the gang, snapping a few pics with them, and listening as Kay recounted the story of how his brother-in-law Suwu had saved his life when he was shot up some years ago, Markio went over and pulled Nikkia to the side.

"That is so nice what you did for your family," she said, taking his face in her hands and looking him right in the eyes. "You really just made me like you a whole lot more."

"I love my family. I'll give 'em the world, if I can."

"Mya's pretty, too. Something off about her, though. She gives off a funny vibe. I don't know if it's because I'm low-key jealous about you fucking her yesterday or what, but I'm just not feeling her at all." She looked out the corner of her eye at Mya, who was busy turning up to a 2 Chainz and Moneybagg Yo song with Tinky and Chanel.

Markio brought a finger up to the side of Nikkia's chin and pushed until her alluring brown eyes were back on his, and he was just about to tell her that he had to head out west to handle something when Bankroll Reese announced to the party that the two limousines he'd ordered had just pulled up outside the hotel. Apparently, before Markio and Nikkia's arrival, everyone had made plans to hit up the Visionary Lounge, Reese's most popular Chicago nightclub, and anyone who didn't want to drive could ride in the limos. Aunt Carolyn and her daughter Rose were the only two who declined to join the club celebration; Aunt Carolyn was sixty-eight, her daughter Rose, fifty, and neither of them were into the whole scene.

Markio had an idea. He smiled when it came to him.

"You drive your car," he said to Nikkia, "and I'll just follow behind you."

"Or I could just ride with you," she countered. "And you need to stop smoking. You're on parole. What if you get drug-tested and fail? I'm not joining the Prison Wives Club."

"I'll be good. But look, I gotta make a quick stop on the way to the club, to handle some'n out west. I'll only take a couple of minutes. I'll be at the club within twenty minutes of y'all pullin' up."

Nikkia squinted at him, tightening her grasp on her hips.

"And my guy Reggie on the way out here with some of my clothes," Markio continued, impervious to Nikkia's intimidating posture. "Any way he could get into that condo you got me moving into? When can I move in? I need the keys. Reggie'll be here any minute."

Nikkia brought out her phone and texted him the address to her Streeterville condo. "I'll call the building manager and have her let him in, and I'll get you a set of keys made first thing tomorrow." She looked up from her phone. "Stay on the phone with me while you 'handle some'n out west,' whatever that means. It better not be another woman."

"Deal," he said, beaming as he lifted his smartphone, which was already ringing with a call from D-Dot. He ignored the call and forwarded the condo address to Reggie. He'd call D-Dot back in a little while. D-Dot was a real hoe-ass nigga, in Markio's opinion, softer than cotton but he was a hustler, and Markio knew he would need all the hustlers he could find in the coming weeks. He had placed an order with Reggie for two hundred pounds of Black Cherry Gelato for 2,000-a-pound, pounds he would sell for $6,000-a-pound, tripling his $400,000 investment.

"I don't want to hear anything about the call dropping or the signal getting weak," Nikkia pressed. "Stay on the phone with me until you meet back up with me."

"I gottchoo, baby. On my mama, I'll stay on the phone with you the whole time."

He stopped by the honeymoon suite and refilled his duffel bag, this time with just two bundles of hundreds, two bundles of fifties, and two bundles of twenties—$170,000.

Ten minutes later, he was in his S-Class Mercedes Benz, driving down Roosevelt Road, en route to his old West Side neighborhood, his only security being the .45 caliber Ruger and whatever was left in his Draco's 50-round banana clip.

Chapter Fourteen

Big Worm poured himself a ball glass of Hennessy on ice and sat alone in the darkness of his living room, illuminated only by the BunnyXXX porn playing on 70-inch television and the screen of his iPad. He was still perusing the comments section below about Nikkia Staples and her "new boo." A few of the comments were interesting. One woman named Shamara Mosley said, '*That's my old boo. Markio Earl, he went to prison in '07 for a body and I ain't seen him since. Nigga got a BIG ASS DICK! I see why she snatched him up.*'

That comment had already gotten over thirteen thousand likes. Several other people who knew Markio had already ratted him out to the black culture mob, tagging his IG page so others could see who he was, and when Worm went to Markio's page the number of followers had risen from just over 3,100 to well over 18,000. Fifteen thousand new followers in a matter of minutes, each one raising the temperature of Worm's blood another full degree.

"This nigga gon die real soon," Worm muttered, and sipped his cognac.

He had on his favorite red Versace robe and a Rolex Sky Dweller wrist watch encrusted with $70,000 in flawless white diamonds. Bam had gotten him a diamond pendant to hang down from the diamond Infinity-link necklace he'd bought for himself before he was shot. The pendant spelled out his nickname in VVS diamonds, which were slightly less expensive than flawless diamonds but no less eye-catching. His vastly sloping belly was wrapped in gauze. His wounds were mostly healed, but there were thin spots in the skin where blood still seeped through to the bandages.

Worm had already concluded that Markio wasn't coming through with the few hundred grand he'd promised. Not that Worm really cared. He had three young shooters on the way to Michigan City to get the motherhood. Then he'd have Markio killed, and when it was all said and done he'd piss on Markio's grave and spit on his headstone.

A bright beam of headlights washed across his living room windows at 10:23 p.m. Worm didn't get up to look until he heard a car door thump shut a minute later, and when he got to the window he looked out and saw a black S-class Mercedes with black rims and pitch black windows. It had parked in front of his candy orange 1964 Chevy Impala convertible, the car he'd been shot in back in April, and Worm knew that the man opening the wrought-iron gate in front of his grandmother's building was Markio because he had on the same outfit from the Instagram video. He was carrying a Louis Vuitton duffel bag in one hand and his phone in the other, the diamonds on his neck twinkling brilliantly in the moonlight.

Worm looked up and down the street, and seeing no one else he wondered how Markio could be so bold as to show up by himself. As if Worm had really let go of the fact that he'd taken a five-million-dollar loss.

"This nigga must think I'm a hoe or some'n," Worm said aloud to himself as he left the window. He grabbed his Kel-Tec 9-millimeter pistol off the end table next to his armchair and slipped into one of the large front pockets of his robe, then went to the side door and unlocked it. "Let him play that tough shit if he wanna," he muttered acidly, "I'll lay him down right here in this apartment, and I don't give a fuck what Bam got to say about that."

***

"So what is it that you want from me?" Nikkia was asking. "I mean you are looking for something long-term, right? Because if you're running game on me I'm gonna be highly upset. You can't just put that kinda dick on a woman and not expect her to need it every day. I will cut you if you even think about leaving me."

Markio cracked up laughing, his eyes darting every which way, searching for signs of an ambush. The Ruger felt heavy in the front of his jeans, and he tried to remember how many bullets were in the clip. He'd chambered a round but he hadn't counted the actual rounds in the magazine since last night, just before he fell asleep on

Reggie's sofa, too high on Percocets, Lean, and blunts of Black Cherry Gelato to remember much of anything.

During the drive from the Four Seasons, he'd forwarded the condo address to Reggie, along with Nikkia's phone number so he could contact her when he got to the address. Then he'd texted Waddell, who said he needed to talk about some business but that he was in Chicago right now and wouldn't be back in MC until sometime tomorrow. When Markio texted back saying that he too was in Chicago, they agreed to link up at The Visionary Lounge.

Now, as Markio walked toward the door on the side of the towering three-floor flat, he began to question Waddell's motive for contacting him. It was just a fleeting thought, but he wondered if the police had also gotten to Waddell. There were certain guys who would really surprise Markio if it came out that they were rats, but Waddell wasn't one of them. If Waddell's younger brother was such a pussy, it wasn't hard to believe that the older brother could possess some of those same traits.

He knocked on the door and looked around again, contemplating drawing his pistol now. Nikkia was going on and on in his ears about how many people were texting her phone and messaging her on Instagram, begging for details about her new flame, but hardly any of it registered in his brain. His mind was keenly focused on Worm, and he couldn't let Nikkia throw him off his square.

"Baby, hold on a minute. I need you to be quiet and just listen," he said.

A second later he heard Worm shout for him to come on in. The door was unlocked.

"What's wrong?" Nikka asked, the excitement in her voice fading away to concern.

"Just be quiet and listen. Switch on that lawyer part of you."

He removed one AirPod from his ear and pocketed it, then used the back of his hand to turn the knob, just as he'd used his knuckle to lift the locking mechanism on the gate and the back of his wrist to turn the knob. No sense in leaving fingerprints at a heroin kingpin's residence.

He pushed open the door with his elbow and stepped inside. All the lights were off, so he waited a couple of seconds for his eyes to adjust to the black. The door opened into the kitchen, and off to the left, at the end of a hallway there was light from a phone or computer tablet, lighting up Worm's face as he sat staring down the hall at Markio.

"You can cut on the light," Worm said. "It's right there next to the door. To your left."

Markio slid his elbow up the wall, flicking three light switches to the *on* position. The kitchen and hallway light switched on, as well as the light outside the door behind him. Markio scanned the kitchen, ready to drop his phone and snatch the Ruger from the front of his waistline. But there was no one waiting for him in the shadows. He elbowed the door shut and walked cautiously down the hallway, glancing into an open bathroom and two bedrooms. No one. In the living room he found Worm sitting alone in a dark-colored leather armchair. There was a porn movie playing on a huge high-definition TV screen, some sexy brown-skinned girl sucking the soul out of a dick.

"Hit that light, too," Worm said, pointing at a switch plate on the living room wall.

"What up, big homie?" Markio knuckled the light switch upward, bathing the room in light.

Unsurprisingly, the living room was furnished with expensive brown leather. A brown fur Louis Vuitton area rug lay beneath a large square block of gray marble that had a slab of glass laid over it—the coffee table. The centerpiece on the slab of glass looked like a gray stone alligator head, and there was a half-empty pint of Wockhardt promethazine with codeine standing next to its snout.

"I ain't think you was gon' show up," Worm said, lighting an overstuffed blunt of something loud. He toked on it. Coughed twice. Toked on it again. "Bam said you would, but I didn't think so."

"I'm a man of my word." Markio sat down on the sofa, placing his duffel on the floor between his shoes and looking up at the TV screen. "Goddamn! Who the fuck is that?"

"That's one of my lil' bops. Bunny triple X. One of the hottest new porn stars in the game. She was in the car with me when I got shot. I paid for her whole body. All that ass, them titties. Took that lil' pooch out her stomach. Even got her teeth done."

Markio tried to focus on Worm, but it was hard. The Bunny girl was the queen of dick sucking. In his ear, Nikkia snickered and said, "This man done built him a whole porn star," and Markio stifled a laugh.

He unzipped the duffel bag and spread it open, showing the cash he had inside it. Then he checked his phone and saw nothing but more Facebook and Instagram notifications. He hadn't realized that Nikkia had over forty million Instagram followers until he'd taken a moment to look at her page when he parked his car out front, and now it seemed like her legions of followers were slowly migrating over to his page. It had taken him five whole years to gain three thousand followers—he'd started his IG page back in 2017, with a smartphone a female guard had smuggled in to him, and yet it had taken less than one hour for his list of followers to grow by more than fifteen thousand.

As if reading Markio's mind, Worm said, "I see that bad bitch you just copped gotcha IG bussin? You know shorty worth like two hundred million?"

"Nah, I didn't know that. She just a girl I always had a crush on. I went to her law firm to hire her and we both happened to be single. I barely even be on social media, and I don't be in the house long enough to watch TV. I be outside, gettin' to the money."

"Man, come on, Lord. So you tellin' me you ain't know she was friends with Alexus."

"Not at all. On my soul. I just want Nikkia 'cause she Nikkia. I ain't know she was famous."

"Well, you hit the jackpot, nigga. Twice. You got my money, then you get the girl. Lucky you." Worm took an even bigger drag on the blunt. The diamonds in his wristwatch sparkled colorfully every time he raised his hand for a puff, as did the ice in his necklace and pendant, and Markio noticed a bulge in the baggy right hand pocket of his robe. "You know, I made over a million dollars today, and Bam say he gon' give me another million. I really don't even need that lil' paper I asked you for."

Markio's phone buzzed with a text message from Tyquan. *'They here.'*

"I'll definitely keep it, "Markio said, staring right at Worm. "I didn't steal nothin' from you, either. Didn't even know it was yours. You should be glad some old white man didn't end up with it."

"I know you didn't steal it," Worm said, and glanced down at his own iPhone. He read something. Then a smile spread across his face. "I just came up again. This time it's a five-million-dollar play so I'm back up seven M's one day. You can't beat that bitch with a bat."

Markio chuckled drably as he rose from the sofa, dropping his phone into the duffel as he stood. "What the fuck did I come over here for then? We good?"

"Aw, we more than good," Worm said, picking up a glass of iced cognac and taking a generous swallow. "Never been better."

Markio snatched the Ruger from his waistline in record time, like a legendary gunslinger in the old west, and he aimed the barrel right at Worm's forehead. Worm was just raising the ball glass of cognac to his mouth for a second swallow when it happened. His hand stopped right below his bearded chin.

"You know the funny thing about drinkin'?" Markio said, lowering his duffel to the floor and moving toward Worm. "You get loud without even meaning to. That's what your dumbass sister Mya did tonight. And guess what? My smartass sister Shakia was right outside the bathroom door, listening to everything Mya told you, and everything you told her, and everything you told Lil' Worm—who, by the way, is about to walk right into three young dumb niggas with nothing to lose and everything to prove." He reached into the pocket of Worm's robe, pulled out a Kel-Tec pistol, and dropped it into his duffel bag, smiling coldly at Worm's burgeoning scowl. "What? You didn't think I would have my people on alert? I feel bad for your son and whoever was dumb enough to get out there with him. They definitely ain't gon' make it back."

In Markio's ear, Nikkia said, "Oh, my God! Markio. What is going on?"

The only answer she got was a deafening gunshot.

Big Worm's head snapped back as the .45 caliber round, traveling at more than eight hundred feet per second, slammed into his forehead, right between the eyebrows, dislodging a large portion of his brain through the back of his skull and splattering it all over the wall behind his chair.

***

Tyquan certainly had something to prove.

The jokes were all over Facebook. He'd been robbed in Coolspring. He'd pissed himself. He'd played hard on social media and then bitched up when the real smoke came his way. And worst of all, he'd let a nigga take his gun, a cardinal sin in the streets.

Now, as he stood nervously in the dark hallway just inside the front door of 1006 West 8th Street in Michigan City, holding the heavy Norinco Mac-90 assault rifle he'd gotten from his uncle Markio's best friend—Reggie—in one sweaty hand and his two-year-old iPhone in the other, watching live footage from his mother's doorbell camera as three young men climbed out of the black Jeep that had been parked out front for the past five minutes, Tyquan was more afraid than ever. His friend Benji stood outside, clutching his raggedy little .25.

"As soon as they open that door," Flocka said, "give it to 'em."

Tyquan nodded. He was scared out of his mind though. He'd been acting like a street nigga ever since he was a teenager, deeply inspired by his uncle Markio's notorious reputation, but the sad truth could not be escaped. Tyquan was no street nigga. He was no killer, no shooter, no trapper. He was just a confused young man who wanted to fit in with the other young gang members, so he'd played the role for years.

Now was his time to show and prove, and the one thing that had him ready to shoot was his shattered reputation and his grim determination to repair it.

Tyquan watched the three men outside as they climbed the porch steps and then pocketed his phone. He raised the Mac-90 and took aim, wiping his damp hands on his black T-shirt. He thought about his mother and grandmother, vacationing in Aruba, and wished he could be there with them instead of here, holding the biggest gun he'd ever held in his life and preparing to pull the trigger. He'd only shot a gun once before, and that had been into the air last New Year's Eve. Was he really ready to shoot an actual person? And not just one man, but three men? He wasn't sure, but as he aimed at the door, looking down the rifle's sights as the doorknob slowly began to turn, he didn't think he had much of a choice.

The door hadn't swung inward two inches when Flocka started firing his Glock, and Benji opened fire right after him, peppering the door with holes. Tyquan pulled the trigger and the Mac-90's recoil caught him off guard, jerking around in his hands as he sprayed the door five feet in front of him. He heard more gunshots coming from outside and saw flashes of gunfire through the windows at the top of the door, but he kept right on shooting, holding the assault rifle firmly in his shaky hands, ignoring the painful sting in his gut he assumed was coming from an intense anxiety attack.

When he finally let up off the trigger, breathing in the pungent air of cordite and gunpowder, he realized the pain in his gut was much more than anxiety related. His stomach was bleeding. His legs were weakening. He touched his shirt and felt the hot wetness just before his knees began to wobble, and he fell sideways against the hallway wall, gasping suddenly short of breath, the rifle weighing him down.

He tried lifting the Mac-90 as Flocka cautiously opened the door with the toe of his shoe, but he was too weak to do it. There were two bodies crumpled on the front porch, and Flocka let off five more shots at the black Jeep as it sped off down the street.

Benji appeared next to Tyquan just as he started sliding down the wall to the tiled hallway floor. His ass landed on several spent shell casings. It was becoming harder to breathe, harder to think. He let go of the Mac-90. Slipped his hand under his shirt and gasped, when his finger slipped into a wet hole an inch below his right side ribcage.

"Tyquan got hit, Flocka," Benji said, casting a worried glance at Flocka.

Flocka was standing over the two men lying on the porch. One of them was still breathing though just barely. Flocka kicked their guns down the concrete porch steps and dialed 9-1-1 on his phone as he stepped back into the hallway.

"Just sit still, Quan. You did good, lil' nigga. Breathe. You'll be a'ight."

***

The Visionary Lounge's second-floor VIP section was lit when Markio walked through the door at 11:00 p.m. on the nose. Tinky and Chanel were standing with Bankroll Reese and his fiancée—Shawnna Wilkins—at the railing overlooking the first-floor stage area, where Louisville rapper EST Gee was performing "Love is Blind," a hit song from his latest studio album. Kay and his brothers were smoking blunts with Rev and Cocky Lord at one of the tables. Chicago rapper Polo G and his Too Turnt Gang occupied three of the fifteen tables, and there were others in the 1,500-square foot VIP room with a whole lot of ice on their necks and wrists who had never seen the inside of a recording booth, including Bam and his girlfriend—Malaysia—both of whom were smoking blunts of exotic weed while enjoying EST Gee's performance from the balcony. Looking at Bam, Markio wondered how long it would be before the news of Worm's death reached him.

Nikkia was sitting at one of the tables, head down, eyes on her phone. Markio went over and sat down next to her. Kissed her on the cheek as she looked up at him and squinted. The music was too loud to talk without either being intimately close or yelling from a distance, so he moved close to her ear and spoke.

"I know it's kinda loud in here. You wanna step outside and talk?"

Her lips moved, but Markio couldn't hear what she said. Then she stood up and walked past him, shouldering her purse and heading toward the rear exit door, which led down a flight of stairs to a big steel door that opened into the rear parking lot. Markio followed her out the door, and halfway down the staircase he grabbed her elbow to stop her.

"What is wrong with you?" Markio asked in his most understanding tone of voice.

"You're what's wrong with me," Nikkia snapped, folding her arms over her chest. "You're not ready for a relationship. You're not ready to leave the streets alone and settle down with a real woman. You got me all charged up to be with you, and then you went and shot somebody while I was on the phone listening."

"He would've killed me," Markio said, a bit more aggressively than he'd intended. "He had just sent his son to harm my family in Michigan City. I just got off the phone with Benji, one of my nephew Tyquan friends. They just shot up my mama's house and shot my nephew in the stomach. That nigga had it coming. Either I was gon' kill him or he was gon' kill me. If you don't believe me, I'll call Benji right now. Better yet, I'll call my sister Shakia, and she'll tell you what she overheard Mya saying in the bathroom earlier tonight."

Nikkia lower lip came out in a pout. Markio thought it looked cute, but he didn't dare say it.

"Let me explain some'n to you," he said. "Some'n you should really know about me." He inhaled and sighed through his nose, getting the words together in his head before he let them out. "I'm a real gangsta, baby. I don't know a better way to describe it than that. Everybody likes to protest about the police killing black men, and they're right, but our biggest enemy lies in our own community. Every man who's ever shot at me or tried to get somebody else to kill me was black just like me, and I put every single one of 'em in the dirt. What would you want me to do in those circumstances? Just let 'em kill me? Would that make you happy?"

She rolled her eyes. Shook her head. "It's my fault. I was hot and horny, and I rushed into this without thinking. Something I never do. Other than my ex-husband, you're the first man I've been with in sixteen years. There are questions I should have asked you. You haven't even met my kids. You haven't even met my parents." "We can all go out for dinner at GAM'S, my treat. Just say the word."

Nikkia shut her eyes and lowered her head. A single tear trickled down from her left eye and she quickly wiped it away. Markio placed his strong brown hands on her waist and rubbed, planting a lasting kiss on her forehead. Her arms went around his back, and she slouched against him.

"Baby, just give me a chance, a'ight? I still had some smoke to clear up in the streets when I walked into your office. Why you think I came in there with a bullet hole in my bankroll? Dude got me shot last night. He had a nigga try to kidnap my ex yesterday, and she shot the lil' nigga in the face. I offered a few hundred thousand dollars to end the whole thing peacefully, and he agreed to it. Then he went and tried to back-door me, and almost got my nephew killed in the process. He got what he was supposed to get in the end. Now I can put all my energy into makin' you happy. That okay?"

She nodded against his chest and pulled back, sniffling. "Oh, damn. I got make-up on your shirt," she said, looking at the spot on his shirt where her face had rested. "I'll have it cleaned and returned to you in the morning. A friend of mine owns a top-of-the-line cleaning service."

"I don't give a fuck about no shirt." Markio kissed her on the lips, his hands creeping around her waist to grab hold of her ass. "I care about you. That's it. I want you to be to me what India Cox is to Durk. What Alexus is to Bulletface. You see all the shit they done been through together? India got to blowin' at some niggas about Durkio. Alexus did the same thing for Bulletface—Several times. I want you to be like that for me."

"I can be that." Nikkia smiled weakly, taking a tissue out of her purse to dab at the undersides of her eyes, "I'm about to leave. I can't be here right now. There's a stripper in VIP who Alexus hates, and I don't wanna be seen around her." She sniffled again. "I just wanna cuddle up in bed with some popcorn and a good movie."

"A'ight, let's go back to the hotel. We can order some popcorn, pick out a good movie to watch, and you can ask me all those questions you feel like you should've asked before." Markio gave her another kiss, gave her ass another tight squeeze, and they descended the staircase the same way they'd entered the Four Seasons, hand-in-hand.

The big black steel door could only be opened from the inside, as it was the entrance most celebrities used to enter the building, and Reese wanted to keep all the crazed fans from barging in on the rich and famous. There were two brawny security guards posted up outside the door, armed with handguns just in case any jack boys attempted to rob the A-list millionaires as they entered or exited the building.

"Her name's Bubbles," Nikkia said, as they continued down the stairs. "The girl Alexus hates. She's in there with Juice, her husband, but she used to be Bulletface's sneaky link."

"Oh, I ain't know that," Markio said. He knew Juice well, had grown up on Trumbull Avenue with him, and he knew that Juice had identical twin daughters, Shawnna and Dawn: two hugely famous Instagram models, one of whom was engaged to Reese, but he hadn't heard of Bubbles.

He pushed open the door and immediately spotted Waddell Flemingston. Waddell was just stepping out of a small red convertible Mustang, wearing a gray Nike jogger that fit his lanky body almost too snugly. Walking Nikkia to her car, which was parked in one of the reserved parking spaces near the door, Markio watched Waddell closely. When Nikkia saw who he was looking at, she leaned in close to him and spoke.

"My firm represented a man named Reginald Prather last year. He's a Black P. Stone who goes by the name of Red Mae. That man you're looking at is the one who wore a wire on him."

"I knew it," Markio said through clenched teeth.

He held open Nikkia's door as she got in, keeping his eyes on Waddell, his casual gaze becoming an ice-cold stare. Waddell was talking on his phone with someone as he walked toward the sidewalk on Laramie, heading around the tall yellow building to join the long line of people waiting to enter through the front doors of the Visionary Lounge on Chicago Avenue.

Markio took out his smart phone and blocked Waddell's phone number, then *FaceTimed* Sway Swanson as he pushed Nikkia's door shut and walked around to his own car, which he'd parked along the passenger's side of Nikkia's Bentley GT convertible.

Sway answered, but Markio could hardly see him through the thick haze of weed smoke, and the sound of music in the background was thunderous. Sway yelled for his sister Stephanie to lower the volume, then he turned his red-veined eyes back to the camera and said, "Bruh, we took care of that nigga Dame. You ain't gon' believe how we caught him. Remember that gay nigga Brandon, who used to stay on Lincoln? Charlene's son?"

Markio nodded as he got in the driver's seat of his Mercedes. "Yeah, what about him?"

"Dame was fuckin with him. You know Brandon go by Trina now. But anyway, Nissa told us Dame was fuckin with a tranny, and she gave us the punk's number. I offered him twenty-five hundred to set Dame up and he went for it. The nigga was suckin' Dame off when Shan jumped in he backseat of Dame's truck. He spit nut all in Dame's face. Shan almost threw up."

Markio only shook his head, leery of saying too much over the phone. With the way the police were sending rats at him, he wasn't in a particularly trusting state of mind.

"Shan let the fag out the truck before he stumped Dame, so he wouldn't have no witness to the murder. I don't think Trina'll say nothin', but you never know the switch make that Glock spit so fast."

"I'll have Reggie slide on y'all when he get back in town," Markio said, meaning he'd have Reggie bring them the $10,000 he'd put on Dame's head. "I gotta go, bruh. Good looking."

"You already know. Just hit us up when you need us. Dub Life, nigga."

Markio connected his iPhone to the car charger and pulled out behind Nikkia, trying to decide who he would contact to get Waddell taken care of. Shannon and Sway had already dropped four bodies for him in the past forty-eight hours. He didn't want to keep pushing the envelope with them. And besides, Waddell was in Chicago, Markio's hometown. Markio didn't need to count on some GD's from Indiana to handle his opps. He had plenty of his own Vice Lords here in the Raq to do that for him, and if it came down to it, he'd do it himself.

Five minutes later, while idling at a red light, he picked up his phone and typed out a text message to his cousin. Buck: '*Lord, a light-skinned nigga named Waddell just got in line in front of the club. He got on a gray jogger with JUST DO IT printed down one leg in white letters. Buddy a rat. He came out here to set me up. I'm leaving, just letting you know what it is.*'

Buck texted back a few seconds later: '*Say less.*' He ended the message with a zipped-lip emoji next to a skull emoji, and it didn't take a rocket scientist to figure out what that meant. Markio wouldn't need to do any more shooting tonight. He had millions of dollars at his disposal now, and men like Buck wouldn't hesitate to handle his dirt for him

Which left Markio with all the time in the world to enjoy with Nikkia Staples.

Chapter Fifteen

Chief Martin Swiztek was behind the desk in his office, going through Markio Earl's social media photos and videos one at a time, searching hungrily for anything of value, when Detective Mulberry knocked on his door. She walked in with the biggest smile on her flushed pink face and sat down across from him, crossing her long legs and saying nothing.

"I take it you've found something. Did Flemingston get the job done?" Swizz asked, sitting forward in his swivel chair and resting his elbows on the desk in front of him. "Please tell me we've got this son of a bitch."

"We've got something," Mulberry said, tossing her silky blond hair. "Okay, so the bad news is we've lost almost every informant I sent after Markio Earl. The only one left is Waddell Flemingston, and since he had to go across state lines we turned him over to the FBI. They wired him up and got him ready. He's supposed to be meeting up with Markio at some night club tonight, and he's absolutely certain he'll get something out of him. That's the closest we've come to getting someone in the same room with Markio since we started this whole investigation."

Swizz nodded, chewing on the end of an ink pen. "It's something," he said. "It may not be a lot, but it's definitely something."

"Oh, there's more," Mulberry said excitedly. Her smile grew, showing the rubber bands stretching from the top of her braces to the bottom. "Okay, you know Damian Middlebrooks was found dead at the Carroll Avenue train station."

Swizz nodded and sat back in his chair, lifting an ankle onto his knee. "Go on."

"Seven or eight gunshot wounds to the right side of the head. Brains blown out the driver's window. But here's something interesting; there was semen on his face, fresh semen, still wet when I arrived on scene. Looked like it was spit on him. And his dick was still hanging out of his pants. We'll be able to collect DNA from the saliva that's mixed with the semen, and that'll give us the identity

of whoever gave him head and spit in his face before he was killed."
She looked to the small yellow notepad she had cupped in one hand
and added, "Oh, and another thing we just got the footage from the
McDonald's surveillance cameras a few blocks down from the train
station, where the initial call was made concerning Damian's
carjacking, and I saw two things. First off, the Buick Roadmaster
the carjacker got out of—we got the plates. Comes back to Michael
Carter, a drug addict who's known around town as Lawnmower
Man. He claims he rented out his car to Sway Swanson, and when
he got it back the front end was damaged. Sway gave him a
thousand dollars for the damages. Coincidentally, the Swanson
brothers and Markio were all members of the Dub Life Gang before
Markio went down for that murder, and the Swanson brothers were
seen on camera visiting Markio's hotel room at the Marriott shortly
after the Cedar Street double homicide. They went in for a few
minutes and left out with huge bulges in their pockets. Rectangular,
cash-shaped bulges."

It was Swizz's turn to smile as he twiddled the ink pen between
two fingers. "Now you're telling me something, Millie! That's what
I'm talking about! Results!"

"And one more thing," Mulberry said, rising from her chair,
jittering with excitement. "You know Ikey Williams, the guy who
was shot by Whitney Clarrett yesterday and crashed that Hellcat
Challenger when he sped off? And Ikey Perkins, the guy who was
left in front of the emergency room at St. Anthony's shortly after
today's murder at Markio's house?"

Swizz held his breath. He'd received authorization from Judge
Lang to bug the hospital room, and he had a strong feeling that
Mulberry was about to reveal something juicy about what the
recording devices had captured.

"We have a clear recording of Williams and Perkins talking
about Markio, and it is everything. Perkins basically confesses to
killing Melvo Crenshaw by accident, thinking Melvo was Markio,
and Williams said Markio got five million dollars of some guy's
drug money out of that storage locker. That's how he's been able to
finance this whole terror campaign against G-Money's crew. It's

why all those guys from Chicago kept coming after him and Whitney Clarrett. We're waiting on an arrest warrant for the Swanson brothers now, and I bet when we get them in custody we'll find their packets stuffed full of cash."

Checking his watch for the time—11:27 p.m.—Swizz got up from his chair, tired from having spent fifteen hours in the office and ready to go home. It seemed like things were finally looking up. His officers and detectives had been working nonstop since G-Money's murder yesterday afternoon, chasing down lead after lead and coming up with nothing, and for a while he'd felt hopeless.

But not anymore. Detective Mulberry had reinvigorated him, breathing new life into his hopeless spirit. He smiled at her as he rounded the desk and gave her a firm, thankful handshake.

"Get home and get yourself some sleep," he said, patting her on the shoulder. "We got some arrests to make first thing tomorrow morning, and I want you there to cuff those bastards when we get there."

Mulberry nodded emphatically, and Swizz started to let go of her hand. But he held on, his brow furrowing as he remembered something she'd said a moment earlier.

"Wait a sec," he said. "The second thing—you said you saw two things on the McDonald's surveillance footage. You didn't tell me what the second thing was."

"Oh, yeah. Whitney Clarrett." Mulberry smacked herself on the forehead. "She was walking out of the McDonald's when Dame was carjacked, and she was with Aaron Fellows, the boy who was with Melvo Crenshaw when he was killed. I'm willing to bet that it was Whitney who put them up to breaking into Markio's house. She knows about that money, and she tried to get those boys to break in and steal it. Only they didn't know that Ikey Perkins and his gang were on their way there to kill Markio over the whole G-Money situation, and Melvo ended up dead."

"Hm." Swizz went to his door and held it open for Mulberry, flicking off his office light and nodding thoughtfully. "We'll need to get Whitney back in here for a second interview. With everything we have on them now, she'll talk. She'll give us everything we need to put Markio Earl in prison for the rest of his miserable life, and I will dance in the streets when the judge throws the book at him."

***

Waddell frowned at his phone, holding it out and examining it as if it were broken. Why wasn't Markio's phone number working? It wouldn't even ring once before going to voicemail.

Shaking his braided head in frustration, Waddell began to text Markio again, but it took him a little longer composing the message than usual because he kept looking up at the three girls standing just ahead of him in line. The three black girls were young and pretty, two light-hued and one dark, all of them with skin-tight dresses and mouthwatering curves. The girl standing directly in front of him had looked back and asked him where he was from. He said Indiana, and she said she was from The Hun'eds which Waddell had heard of but never visited. He'd asked for her phone number and she'd swiftly declined, claiming to have a controlling boyfriend at home, but he knew it was a hard curve. She was here looking for a baller, and Waddell had eighty-two dollars in his pocket.

But he wouldn't be broke for long. The two federal agents who'd wired him up with an audio recorder and a pair of sunglasses with a camera hidden in them had explained that if he get Markio Earl to confess to his involvement in any of the Michigan City murders, he would not only receive the $10,000 reward from the Michigan City Police Department but also a $25,000 reward from the FBI. Waddell would use the money for good, to buy a house for his family so they could move out of the musty old two-bedroom apartment they lived in now, and he'd no doubt invest at least $10,000 into opening the shoe store he'd always dreamed of owning. Then all little bitches like the yellowbone standing in front of him would be all on his dick, and he'd be the one doing the hard curving.

He went back to typing. '*Markio, wussup lil' bro? I'm almost at the door, u n there or what?*' His thumb was hovering over the send button when the most surprising thing happened: his smart phone was snatched right out of his hand. He looked up, saw a fleeing man with a red hoodie covering his head running off down Chicago Avenue, and immediately gave chase.

The boy was fast. He rounded the corner onto Laramie and kept running, looking back at Waddell as they ran alongside the enormous building. They passed the rear parking lot and continued on past the two clapboard houses that stood just beyond it. Waddell was on him, but Waddell was forty, and a lifetime of smoking and never hitting the gym took its toll very quickly. He made it to the fourth house and had to stop, bending over and clutching his knees as he winced against a sharp pain in his side and struggled to catch his breath.

Raising his head, Waddell was surprised to see that the boy in the red hoodie had also stopped running. In fact, the boy was walking back toward Waddell, holding the phone out to him and smiling.

Waddell straightened and started walking toward the boy, suddenly hoping the nondescript FBI van that had sat in to get wired up was somewhere nearby, watching this whole scene play out.

"I was fuckin' with you, joe," the boy said, and laughed.

Waddell faked a smile, but he was going to pound this young nigga's face in as soon as he got close enough to do it. They were twenty feet away from each other, Waddell passing the fifth house now, his lungs expanding and deflating his mind racing.

And then the boy stopped. Reaching under his hoodie, he pulled out a black handgun with a 30 round clip sticking out of its handle. Waddell's eyes went wide, and before he even had a chance to turn and run, the repeated sting of fully automatic gunfire pelting his chest and abdomen knocked him off his feet.

Suddenly he was looking up at the star spangled sky above, blinking rapidly, trying to breathe and finding only liquid in his lungs, like he was breathing underwater. The boy appeared over him, no longer wearing a smile, and aimed the gun at his face.

The gun flashed, and Waddell Flemingston ceased to exist at precisely 11:41 p.m.

***

The time was 11:42 p.m. when Markio and Nikkia walked into the honeymoon suite at the Four Seasons. He'd been on the phone with her for most of the ride here, listening as she described her favorite getaway destination (the Costilla Resort and Hotel in Cancun, Mexico), her favorite designers of the moment (Fendi, Prada, and Chanel), and even her favorite brand of popcorn (Garrett's). Apparently, this kind of knowledge was important to relationships, so he listened attentively, doing his best to keep his mind off all the blood that had been spilled in the streets over the last forty-eight hours.

While Nikkia phoned room service and ordered popcorn (the hotel happened to have Garrett's popcorn in its kitchen, "See!" Nikkia shrieked. "Everybody eats Garrett's!), Markio shucked off his shoes, dropped his duffel next to his other three duffels, and climbed into bed, picking up the TV remote to surf through the channel guide for a movie.

Nikkia disappeared into the bathroom again. "Don't start the movie without me!" she yelled, and when she came out a few minutes later, wearing a see-through red lace bra and matching thong panties, Markio's eyes lit up.

"Yeah, ain't no way in hell I'ma be able to focus on no movie when you're dressed like that," he said.

"Well, you'll have to. My poor little coochie is way too sore right now." She joined him in bed, and he handed her the remote so she could search for a movie while he used his phone to scroll through the notifications on his Instagram page. He was up to 29,700 followers now, and he couldn't believe it.

He left IG and went to his text messages to delete the thread between him and Buck, just in case the police got onto him about the text he'd sent about Waddell. Which made him think of something he'd been meaning to ask Nikkia all day.

"I got a question," he said. "You know how a lot of people say it's okay to talk about whatever on *FaceTime*, 'cause the Feds can't record it? Is that true?"

"Absolutely not. That's how they just indicted Young Thug and his crew. *FaceTime* calls aren't recorded, but state and federal authorities can subpoena *Apple* for access to your *FaceTime* calls if they have cause to believe you're involved in some sort of criminal conspiracy, and they can record video of the calls or watch them live as you're making them. Now, the data—that's recorded. Every text message you send and receive is recorded data, so be careful not to say anything incriminating in your text messages, especially if you feel like there's a chance the police could be investigating you."

Markio's eyes lit up again, and he decided he'd switch phones first thing tomorrow.

He looked at a video message from Reggie that showed Reggie and his baby mama, Tootie, walking around inside the Streeterville condo, the eight stainless steel suitcases standing in a large walk-in closet in one of the most spacious bedrooms Markio had ever seen. "This it right here, bruh," Reggie said, sweeping the camera around the huge living room. "Me and Tootie stayin' here tonight. Fuck what you heard. We in this bitch like it's AirBnB."

Markio chucked and wrote: '*Go on and stay. Y'all have fun. I'll be through there in the a.m.*'

By the time the popcorn and other snacks and beverages arrived, Nikkia had settled on *Creed II*, and Markio had deleted the photos and videos with Whitney in them from his Instagram page. Nikkia had been checking her own IG page every minute or so, and when Markio finished deleting all the signs of Whitney from his page, he witnessed Nikkia's spirits brighten almost instantly. She breathed a heavy sigh of relief and rested her head on his shoulder.

"Take off this shirt. We're in bed. You don't wear street clothes to bed," she said, after a time, and she raised her cheek from his shoulder until the two-thousand-dollar shirt was off, tossed aside along with his jeans.

Underneath the covers, she traced his abs with her fingernails. When Michael B. Jordan began training for his next big fight on the TV screen, Nikkia's restless fingers crept down into Markio's boxer-briefs. He'd been thinking about Mya when those delicate fingers closed around his already semi-erect penis, wondering if his sister Shakia was already stomping her teeth out for attempting to set him up, but as Nikkia began to rub and pull on his growing erection, all thoughts of Mya vanished from his mind. He turned his head and planted a soft kiss on Nikkia's shoulder.

"What was that porn star's name again?" she asked, and Markio immediately knew who she was talking about.

"BunnyXXX," he said, delivering another kiss to her shoulder as he removed his boxer-briefs under the covers and threw them over the bedside.

Nikkia brought up Pornhub on the smart TV and quickly found the porn star's page. There were numerous videos. She pressed *play* on one that was captioned 'Throat Goat Action in Barbados,' and within seconds the two of them were gawking at the beautiful brown-hued girl's phenomenal oral skills.

"Daaaamn!" Nikkia said in fluctuating tones of amazement, "How in the world can she fit all that down her throat? And look at how wet her mouth is. I don't even think my mouth can produce that much spit. It's like a hurricane in her mouth."

"Well," Markio said smilingly, "let's see what kinda storm you got in yours."

She gave him a watchful side-eye, the corner of her mouth pulling back and rising in a devilish little smirk. "As long as you give me that tornado tongue you got in yours."

"What we waitin' for, then?" Markio kissed her sumptuous lips, glancing at the BunnyXXX porn in his periphery and wishing he could receive that kind of head from Nikkia, but he'd settle for whatever kind of head Nikkia had in her arsenal.

She got up and threw a knee over his face, slowly lowering herself down onto him in the sixty-nine position and pushing back the covers, and Markio fingered her sexy red panties to the side and went to town, licking and sucking on her pretty pussy before she'd even touched his dick. He loved the sweet and juicy taste of her. He smacked her on the ass, inhaling deeply not because he needed a breath but because he craved the luscious scent of her.

He was tempted to say something when he realized she had yet to even touch his throbbing erection, but he was too into what he was doing to speak, and she was too into what he was doing to do anything but moan, so he went on doing it until she came all over his probing tongue, her big butt cheeks quivering on his face, smothering him.

"Oh, my God, Markio. You are so good with that tongue of yours."

"You better put that hurricane to work," he said, and delivered a sharp smack to her left buttock as he went back to sucking on her dripping-wet vaginal lips.

Nikkia leaned forward, arching her back. She lifted his dick from his rock-hard abdomen and took it into her mouth, and as she began to go up and down, bobbing her head in sync with the Beyonce song playing in the background of the bunny XXX porn video, Markio realized that Nikkia was a lot better at sucking dick then she'd let on. She'd sneaked some kind of black rubber vibrating rose out of her purse and was using it on his balls as she sucked and slurped and choked herself on his nearly eleven-inch-long erection.

At first he thought the Percocets in his system would lead to another two-hour wait before he ejaculated but the dual sensation of Nikkia's slurping mouth and the vibrating sex toy on his nuts sent him over the edge in under five minutes. Nikkia sucked on just the head as it spewed out a copious load of cum, and he heard her throat muscle contracting as she gulped it all down in four large swallows.

Markio dropped his head back onto the pillow, a contented grin on his shiny wet mouth. If this was a hint of what life with Nikkia Staples was going to be like, he was ready to sign a thirty-year lease.

He sat up on his elbows as she crawled hurriedly over to her side of the bed and snatched a bottled water off the snack tray. She cracked it open and drank thirstily, her pretty face twisted in disgust.

"That was just too much," she said, and drank some more, fanning her face dramatically. "Ugh, it's still stuck in my throat. I feel like I just drank a protein shake. You come like a fucking horse."

Markio burst out laughing. *Yeah*, he thought, *this thing with Nikkia is going to be fun.*

Chapter Sixteen

Whitney had given her sister—Candace—a thousand dollars to watch over her four children while she was away for the weekend, and she'd also given the kids a thousand dollars each. The rest of the cash she'd stored beneath two loose floorboards in her bedroom closet. She planned to use the remaining $40,000 trying to bring iKiss Cosmetics to store shelves nationwide, but if this whole deal with Bunny worked out, she'd be able to do a lot more than that and likely a whole lot sooner.

Just to be sure that nothing shady was in the works, she'd made Bunny *FaceTime* her before she boarded the United Airlines flight from Chicago to Miami. In the video chat, she'd seen Keondre Muck and his teammate Justin Fisher throwing a football back and forth across a massive green lawn behind a huge greystone mansion, and then Bunny had given her a video tour of the mansion's luxurious interior. Just the sight of it all had made Whitney's heart stop—okay, maybe not literally, but that's certainly what it felt like, especially when she got a glimpse of the wall of water that fell from the high ceiling in the dining room into a pond separating the large room from the kitchen.

And now, as she and the other first-class passengers were escorted off the passenger jet, she was over the moon to see Bunny standing next to the open rear passenger door of a black Rolls-Royce Phantom.

"Yay! My abuser!" Bunny yelled jokingly, and Whitney gave her a tight look before they both fell into a burst of tension-relieving laughter.

Bunny was dressed in head-to-toe Fendi: a bucket hat, a skin-tight mini dress, a shoulder bag, and knee-high boots. She wore a diamond Cartier watch on one wrist and a diamond tennis bracelet on the other. Her curves looked even more jaw-dropping than they had when Whitney and Eva had kicked her ass in the hospital parking lot. She wrapped her arms around Whitney, hugging her as if they were long lost friends, and when she pulled back she asked, "So, what all did you bring?"

Whitney held up her brand-new Chanel bag. "This is it. I have my bank card and a couple of credit cards but I didn't pack anything. I'll buy a couple of summer dresses to wear while I'm down here."

"No, girl. With a body like that, you need bathing suits. Bikinis. That'll get you all the attention you need from Keondre and his teammates, and I brought plenty for you to choose from."

They slipped into the back of the Phantom. A dark-skinned male chauffeur with thick dreadlocks shut the door for them, and Bunny closed the curtains over their windows. She had a bottle of Bel Air Rose waiting, along with two champagne glasses, and as she popped open the bottle, she looked over at Whitney and smiled. There was some light bruising beneath the makeup under her left eye, but aside from that she looked fine. She actually looked more than fine. She looked breathtaking.

"I talked to Worm a little while ago," Bunny said. "He was waiting on Markio to pull up on him, and he was pissed. I guess Markio's all over the internet with that famous lawyer chick, Nikkia Staples, a woman whose net worth is about fifty times the amount of money Markio got from Worm."

Whitney tried and failed to hide her disdain. She was well aware of the Instagram live video. Candace had texted her about it. Her daughter—Eva—had texted her the link to the video. About twenty of her friends had tagged her under Nikkia's video. And to make it even worse, Whitney and Nikkia knew each other well. They'd gone to school together, and had dated the same guy—an older man named Tommy Hodgkins—back in their teenage years. The fact that Nikkia would hook up with Markio without so much as a courtesy text had Whitney on fifty.

"I'll tell you something you may not know about Keondre Muck," Bunny said as she handed Whitney a glass of champagne. "He's from Little Haiti, and his brother— Voltaire—is the head of the Zoe Pound until Ali comes home from the Feds. Get in good with Voltaire, and whenever you feel like getting some payback for all the wrong Markio's done to you, just tell him about it. He'll make Markio wish he was never born, and if you tell Voltaire about that five million dollars, he'll do it a whole lot sooner."

Whitney nodded thoughtfully, sipping her champagne and thinking over the vengeful proposition. She brought out her iPhone and took another look at Markio's Instagram page, and when she saw that he had deleted all signs of her from his photos and videos, a hate-fueled fire ignited in her heart, a blazing conflagration that swept through her entire being like an Arizona wildfire.

"I think you might be onto something," she said, staring coldly at the rising bubbles in her glass. "Introduce me to Voltaire."

To Be Continued...
Super Gremlin 3
Coming Soon

King Rio

Lock Down Publications and Ca$h Presents assisted

publishing packages.

BASIC PACKAGE $499

Editing

Cover Design

Formatting

UPGRADED PACKAGE $800

Typing

Editing

Cover Design

Formatting

ADVANCE PACKAGE $1,200

Super Gremlin 2

Typing

Editing

Cover Design

Formatting

Copyright registration

Proofreading

Upload book to Amazon

LDP SUPREME PACKAGE $1,500

Typing

Editing

Cover Design

Formatting

Copyright registration

King Rio

Proofreading

Set up Amazon account

Upload book to Amazon

Advertise on LDP Amazon and Facebook page

***Other services available upon request. Additional

charges may apply

Lock Down Publications

P.O. Box 944

Stockbridge, GA 30281-9998

Phone # 470 303-9761

Submission Guideline

Submit the first three chapters of your completed

manuscript to ldpsubmissions@gmail.com,

subject line: Your book's title. The manuscript

must be in a .doc file and sent as an attachment.

Document should be in Times New Roman,

double spaced and in size 12 font. Also, provide

your synopsis and full contact information. If

sending multiple submissions, they must each be

in a separate email.

Have a story but no way to send it electronically?

You can still submit to LDP/Ca$h Presents. Send

in the first three chapters, written or typed, of your

completed manuscript to:

LDP: Submissions Dept

King Rio

Po Box 944

Stockbridge, Ga 30281

DO NOT send original manuscript. Must be a duplicate.

Provide your synopsis and a cover letter containing your full contact information.

Thanks for considering LDP and Ca$h Presents.

NEW RELEASES

SALUTE MY SAVAGERY by FUMIYA PAYNE

THE COCAINE PRINCESS 10 by KING RIO

CONFESSIONS OF A JACKBOY 3 by NICHOLAS LOCK

SUPER GREMLIN 2 by KING RIO

Coming Soon from Lock Down Publications/Ca$h Presents
BLOOD OF A BOSS **VI**
SHADOWS OF THE GAME II
TRAP BASTARD II
By **Askari**
LOYAL TO THE GAME **IV**
By **T.J. & Jelissa**
TRUE SAVAGE **VIII**
MIDNIGHT CARTEL IV
DOPE BOY MAGIC IV
CITY OF KINGZ III
NIGHTMARE ON SILENT AVE II
THE PLUG OF LIL MEXICO III
CLASSIC CITY II
By **Chris Green**
BLAST FOR ME **III**
A SAVAGE DOPEBOY III
CUTTHROAT MAFIA III
DUFFLE BAG CARTEL VII
HEARTLESS GOON VI
By **Ghost**
A HUSTLER'S DECEIT III
KILL ZONE II
BAE BELONGS TO ME III
TIL DEATH II
By **Aryanna**
KING OF THE TRAP III
By **T.J. Edwards**
GORILLAZ IN THE BAY V
3X KRAZY III

STRAIGHT BEAST MODE III

De'Kari

KINGPIN KILLAZ IV

STREET KINGS III

PAID IN BLOOD III

CARTEL KILLAZ IV

DOPE GODS III

Hood Rich

SINS OF A HUSTLA II

ASAD

YAYO V

Bred In The Game 2

S. Allen

THE STREETS WILL TALK II

By Yolanda Moore

SON OF A DOPE FIEND III

HEAVEN GOT A GHETTO III

SKI MASK MONEY III

By Renta

LOYALTY AIN'T PROMISED III

By Keith Williams

I'M NOTHING WITHOUT HIS LOVE II

SINS OF A THUG II

TO THE THUG I LOVED BEFORE II

IN A HUSTLER I TRUST II

By Monet Dragun

QUIET MONEY IV

EXTENDED CLIP III

THUG LIFE IV

By **Trai'Quan**

THE STREETS MADE ME IV

By **Larry D. Wright**

IF YOU CROSS ME ONCE III

ANGEL V

By **Anthony Fields**

THE STREETS WILL NEVER CLOSE IV

By **K'ajji**

HARD AND RUTHLESS III

KILLA KOUNTY IV

By **Khufu**

MONEY GAME III

By **Smoove Dolla**

JACK BOYS VS DOPE BOYS IV

A GANGSTA'S QUR'AN V

COKE GIRLZ II

COKE BOYS II

LIFE OF A SAVAGE V

CHI'RAQ GANGSTAS V

SOSA GANG IV

BRONX SAVAGES II

BODYMORE KINGPINS II

BLOOD OF A GOON II

By **Romell Tukes**

MURDA WAS THE CASE III

Elijah R. Freeman

AN UNFORESEEN LOVE IV

BABY, I'M WINTERTIME COLD III

By **Meesha**

QUEEN OF THE ZOO III

Super Gremlin 2

By **Black Migo**

KING KILLA II

By Vincent "Vitto" Holloway

BETRAYAL OF A THUG III

By Fre$h

THE BIRTH OF A GANGSTER IV

By Delmont Player

TREAL LOVE II

By Le'Monica Jackson

FOR THE LOVE OF BLOOD IV

By Jamel Mitchell

RAN OFF ON DA PLUG II

By Paper Boi Rari

HOOD CONSIGLIERE III

By Keese

PRETTY GIRLS DO NASTY THINGS II

By Nicole Goosby

LOVE IN THE TRENCHES II

By Corey Robinson

FOREVER GANGSTA III

By Adrian Dulan

SUPER GREMLIN III

By King Rio

CRIME BOSS II

Playa Ray

LOYALTY IS EVERYTHING III

Molotti

HERE TODAY GONE TOMORROW II

By Fly Rock

REAL G'S MOVE IN SILENCE II

King Rio

By Von Diesel
GRIMEY WAYS IV
By Ray Vinci
BLOOD AND GAMES II
By King Dream
THE BLACK DIAMOND CARTEL II
By SayNoMore

<u>**Available Now**</u>

RESTRAINING ORDER **I & II**
By **CA$H & Coffee**
LOVE KNOWS NO BOUNDARIES **I II & III**
By **Coffee**
RAISED AS A GOON I, II, III & IV
BRED BY THE SLUMS I, II, III
BLAST FOR ME I & II
ROTTEN TO THE CORE I II III
A BRONX TALE I, II, III
DUFFLE BAG CARTEL I II III IV V VI
HEARTLESS GOON I II III IV V
A SAVAGE DOPEBOY I II
DRUG LORDS I II III
CUTTHROAT MAFIA I II
KING OF THE TRENCHES

By **Ghost**

LAY IT DOWN **I & II**

LAST OF A DYING BREED I II

BLOOD STAINS OF A SHOTTA I & II III

By **Jamaica**

LOYAL TO THE GAME I II III

LIFE OF SIN I, II III

By **TJ & Jelissa**

BLOODY COMMAS I & II

SKI MASK CARTEL I II & III

KING OF NEW YORK I II,III IV V

RISE TO POWER I II III

COKE KINGS I II III IV V

BORN HEARTLESS I II III IV

KING OF THE TRAP I II

By **T.J. Edwards**

IF LOVING HIM IS WRONG...I & II

LOVE ME EVEN WHEN IT HURTS I II III

By **Jelissa**

WHEN THE STREETS CLAP BACK I & II III

THE HEART OF A SAVAGE I II III IV

MONEY MAFIA I II

LOYAL TO THE SOIL I II III

By **Jibril Williams**

A DISTINGUISHED THUG STOLE MY HEART I II & III

LOVE SHOULDN'T HURT I II III IV

RENEGADE BOYS I II III IV

PAID IN KARMA I II III

SAVAGE STORMS I II III

AN UNFORESEEN LOVE I II III

BABY, I'M WINTERTIME COLD I II

By **Meesha**

A GANGSTER'S CODE I &, II III

A GANGSTER'S SYN I II III

THE SAVAGE LIFE I II III

CHAINED TO THE STREETS I II III

BLOOD ON THE MONEY I II III

A GANGSTA'S PAIN I II III

By J-Blunt

PUSH IT TO THE LIMIT

By **Bre' Hayes**

BLOOD OF A BOSS **I, II, III, IV, V**

SHADOWS OF THE GAME

TRAP BASTARD

By **Askari**

THE STREETS BLEED MURDER **I, II & III**

THE HEART OF A GANGSTA I II& III

By **Jerry Jackson**

CUM FOR ME I II III IV V VI VII VIII

An **LDP Erotica Collaboration**

BRIDE OF A HUSTLA **I II & II**

THE FETTI GIRLS **I, II& III**

CORRUPTED BY A GANGSTA I, II III, IV

BLINDED BY HIS LOVE

THE PRICE YOU PAY FOR LOVE I, II ,III

DOPE GIRL MAGIC I II III

By **Destiny Skai**

WHEN A GOOD GIRL GOES BAD

By **Adrienne**

THE COST OF LOYALTY I II III

Super Gremlin 2

By Kweli

A GANGSTER'S REVENGE **I II III & IV**

THE BOSS MAN'S DAUGHTERS I II III IV V

A SAVAGE LOVE **I & II**

BAE BELONGS TO ME I II

A HUSTLER'S DECEIT I, II, III

WHAT BAD BITCHES DO I, II, III

SOUL OF A MONSTER I II III

KILL ZONE

A DOPE BOY'S QUEEN I II III

TIL DEATH

By **Aryanna**

A KINGPIN'S AMBITON

A KINGPIN'S AMBITION **II**

I MURDER FOR THE DOUGH

By **Ambitious**

TRUE SAVAGE I II III IV V VI VII

DOPE BOY MAGIC I, II, III

MIDNIGHT CARTEL I II III

CITY OF KINGZ I II

NIGHTMARE ON SILENT AVE

THE PLUG OF LIL MEXICO I II

CLASSIC CITY

By **Chris Green**

A DOPEBOY'S PRAYER

By **Eddie "Wolf" Lee**

THE KING CARTEL **I, II & III**

By **Frank Gresham**

THESE NIGGAS AIN'T LOYAL **I, II & III**

By **Nikki Tee**

King Rio

GANGSTA SHYT **I II &III**

By **CATO**

THE ULTIMATE BETRAYAL

By **Phoenix**

BOSS'N UP **I , II & III**

By **Royal Nicole**

I LOVE YOU TO DEATH

By **Destiny J**

I RIDE FOR MY HITTA

I STILL RIDE FOR MY HITTA

By **Misty Holt**

LOVE & CHASIN' PAPER

By **Qay Crockett**

TO DIE IN VAIN

SINS OF A HUSTLA

By **ASAD**

BROOKLYN HUSTLAZ

By **Boogsy Morina**

BROOKLYN ON LOCK I & II

By **Sonovia**

GANGSTA CITY

By **Teddy Duke**

A DRUG KING AND HIS DIAMOND I & II III

A DOPEMAN'S RICHES

HER MAN, MINE'S TOO I, II

CASH MONEY HO'S

THE WIFEY I USED TO BE I II

PRETTY GIRLS DO NASTY THINGS

By Nicole Goosby

TRAPHOUSE KING **I II & III**

178

KINGPIN KILLAZ I II III

STREET KINGS I II

PAID IN BLOOD **I II**

CARTEL KILLAZ I II III

DOPE GODS I II

By **Hood Rich**

LIPSTICK KILLAH **I, II, III**

CRIME OF PASSION I II & III

FRIEND OR FOE I II III

By **Mimi**

STEADY MOBBN' **I, II, III**

THE STREETS STAINED MY SOUL I II III

By **Marcellus Allen**

WHO SHOT YA **I, II, III**

SON OF A DOPE FIEND I II

HEAVEN GOT A GHETTO I II

SKI MASK MONEY I II

Renta

GORILLAZ IN THE BAY **I II III IV**

TEARS OF A GANGSTA I II

3X KRAZY I II

STRAIGHT BEAST MODE I II

DE'KARI

TRIGGADALE I II III

MURDAROBER WAS THE CASE I II

Elijah R. Freeman

GOD BLESS THE TRAPPERS I, II, III

THESE SCANDALOUS STREETS I, II, III

FEAR MY GANGSTA I, II, III IV, V

THESE STREETS DON'T LOVE NOBODY I, II

BURY ME A G I, II, III, IV, V

A GANGSTA'S EMPIRE I, II, III, IV

THE DOPEMAN'S BODYGAURD I II

THE REALEST KILLAZ I II III

THE LAST OF THE OGS I II III

Tranay Adams

THE STREETS ARE CALLING

Duquie Wilson

MARRIED TO A BOSS I II III

By Destiny Skai & Chris Green

KINGZ OF THE GAME I II III IV V VI VII

CRIME BOSS

Playa Ray

SLAUGHTER GANG I II III

RUTHLESS HEART I II III

By Willie Slaughter

FUK SHYT

By Blakk Diamond

DON'T F#CK WITH MY HEART I II

By Linnea

ADDICTED TO THE DRAMA I II III

IN THE ARM OF HIS BOSS II

By Jamila

YAYO I II III IV

A SHOOTER'S AMBITION I II

BRED IN THE GAME

By S. Allen

TRAP GOD I II III

RICH $AVAGE I II III

MONEY IN THE GRAVE I II III

Super Gremlin 2

By Martell Troublesome Bolden
FOREVER GANGSTA I II
GLOCKS ON SATIN SHEETS I II
By Adrian Dulan
TOE TAGZ I II III IV
LEVELS TO THIS SHYT I II
IT'S JUST ME AND YOU I II
By Ah'Million
KINGPIN DREAMS I II III
RAN OFF ON DA PLUG
By Paper Boi Rari
CONFESSIONS OF A GANGSTA I II III IV
CONFESSIONS OF A JACKBOY I II III
By Nicholas Lock
I'M NOTHING WITHOUT HIS LOVE
SINS OF A THUG
TO THE THUG I LOVED BEFORE
A GANGSTA SAVED XMAS
IN A HUSTLER I TRUST
By Monet Dragun
CAUGHT UP IN THE LIFE I II III
THE STREETS NEVER LET GO I II III
By Robert Baptiste
NEW TO THE GAME I II III
MONEY, MURDER & MEMORIES I II III
By **Malik D. Rice**
LIFE OF A SAVAGE I II III IV
A GANGSTA'S QUR'AN I II III IV
MURDA SEASON I II III
GANGLAND CARTEL I II III

King Rio

CHI'RAQ GANGSTAS I II III IV

KILLERS ON ELM STREET I II III

JACK BOYZ N DA BRONX I II III

A DOPEBOY'S DREAM I II III

JACK BOYS VS DOPE BOYS I II III

COKE GIRLZ

COKE BOYS

SOSA GANG I II III

BRONX SAVAGES

BODYMORE KINGPINS

BLOOD OF A GOON

By Romell Tukes

LOYALTY AIN'T PROMISED I II

By Keith Williams

QUIET MONEY I II III

THUG LIFE I II III

EXTENDED CLIP I II

A GANGSTA'S PARADISE

By **Trai'Quan**

THE STREETS MADE ME I II III

By **Larry D. Wright**

THE ULTIMATE SACRIFICE I, II, III, IV, V, VI

KHADIFI

IF YOU CROSS ME ONCE I II

ANGEL I II III IV

IN THE BLINK OF AN EYE

By **Anthony Fields**

THE LIFE OF A HOOD STAR

By Ca$h & Rashia Wilson

THE STREETS WILL NEVER CLOSE I II III

182

Super Gremlin 2

By K'ajji

CREAM I II III

THE STREETS WILL TALK

By Yolanda Moore

NIGHTMARES OF A HUSTLA I II III

BLOOD AND GAMES

By King Dream

CONCRETE KILLA I II III

VICIOUS LOYALTY I II III

By Kingpen

HARD AND RUTHLESS I II

MOB TOWN 251

THE BILLIONAIRE BENTLEYS I II III

REAL G'S MOVE IN SILENCE

By Von Diesel

GHOST MOB

Stilloan Robinson

MOB TIES I II III IV V VI

SOUL OF A HUSTLER, HEART OF A KILLER I II III

GORILLAZ IN THE TRENCHES I II III

THE BLACK DIAMOND CARTEL

By SayNoMore

BODYMORE MURDERLAND I II III

THE BIRTH OF A GANGSTER I II III

By Delmont Player

FOR THE LOVE OF A BOSS

By C. D. Blue

MOBBED UP I II III IV

THE BRICK MAN I II III IV V

THE COCAINE PRINCESS I II III IV V VI VII VIII IX X

King Rio

SUPER GREMLIN I II
By King Rio
KILLA KOUNTY I II III IV
By Khufu
MONEY GAME I II
By Smoove Dolla
A GANGSTA'S KARMA I II III
By FLAME
KING OF THE TRENCHES I II III
by **GHOST & TRANAY ADAMS**
QUEEN OF THE ZOO I II
By **Black Migo**
GRIMEY WAYS I II III
By Ray Vinci
XMAS WITH AN ATL SHOOTER
By Ca$h & Destiny Skai
KING KILLA
By Vincent "Vitto" Holloway
BETRAYAL OF A THUG I II
By Fre$h
THE MURDER QUEENS I II III
By Michael Gallon
TREAL LOVE
By Le'Monica Jackson
FOR THE LOVE OF BLOOD I II III
By Jamel Mitchell
HOOD CONSIGLIERE I II
By Keese
PROTÉGÉ OF A LEGEND I II III
LOVE IN THE TRENCHES

Super Gremlin 2

By Corey Robinson

BORN IN THE GRAVE I II III

By Self Made Tay

MOAN IN MY MOUTH

SANCTIFIED AND HORNY

By XTASY

TORN BETWEEN A GANGSTER AND A GENTLEMAN

By J-BLUNT & Miss Kim

LOYALTY IS EVERYTHING I II

Molotti

HERE TODAY GONE TOMORROW

By Fly Rock

PILLOW PRINCESS

By S. Hawkins

NAÏVE TO THE STREETS

WOMEN LIE MEN LIE I II III

GIRLS FALL LIKE DOMINOS

STACK BEFORE YOU SPURLGE

FIFTY SHADES OF SNOW I II III

By A. Roy Milligan

SALUTE MY SAVAGERY I II

By Fumiya Payne

BOOKS BY LDP'S CEO, CA$H

TRUST IN NO MAN

TRUST IN NO MAN 2

TRUST IN NO MAN 3

BONDED BY BLOOD

SHORTY GOT A THUG

THUGS CRY

THUGS CRY 2

THUGS CRY 3

TRUST NO BITCH

TRUST NO BITCH 2

TRUST NO BITCH 3

TIL MY CASKET DROPS

RESTRAINING ORDER

RESTRAINING ORDER 2

IN LOVE WITH A CONVICT

LIFE OF A HOOD STAR

XMAS WITH AN ATL SHOOTER

Super Gremlin 2

www.ingramcontent.com/pod-product-compliance
Lightning Source LLC
Chambersburg PA
CBHW071211260626
47162CB00004B/1262